COVER BLOWN

Covert police work clashes with a murder investigation

IAN ROBINSON

THE
BOOK
FOLKS

Published by The Book Folks

London, 2021

© Ian Robinson

ISBN 978-1-913516-78-9

www.thebookfolks.com

Cover Blown is the second standalone title in the DI Pippa Nash and DS Nick Moretti mystery series.

'No way. I'm not taking it home,' came his reply.

'It needs a new home now, JJ, and look at you… you're a natural cat person…' Moretti said, his smile hidden by his face shield.

'The cat will go to the RSPCA until we can establish if a family member will take her,' Nash said. 'Stick it in a spare exhibit crate but make it comfortable. We don't want to lose it. Get one of the inside team to contact the RSPCA and they can pick it up.'

Moretti found a towel and some toys and placed them in the crate before JJ gently placed the cat inside and closed over the lid. He left a gap for the cat to breathe as he taped the lid in place.

The bedroom they were in had been used for storage. It contained a single bed, a desk, and a gap where the victim's laptop had sat before they'd bagged it up. This is how a victim's life became once Nash's team arrived. Their sanctuary invaded, yet again, by unwanted visitors. Nash would ensure they examined every minutiae of the victim's lifestyle in an effort to establish who she was, who had killed her, and why. Intention, mind-set and motive were the key elements in any successful prosecution and that was her team's ultimate goal.

She checked her watch, an old Rolex left to her by her mum. It showed 10 p.m. A good time for her house-to-house detectives to catch people at home. They may have seen or heard something suspicious. She knew it was the type of building where people would come and go at odd times. You couldn't live here without money, and with money came a certain lifestyle that rarely saw people at home. This would be an issue in tracing any witnesses. She hoped the camera system employed in the block would provide a lead. Nash waited for Dr King to surface from the bathroom and provide her with an idea as to time and cause of death.

CHAPTER TWO

Dr King vacated the bathroom and Nash and Moretti joined him in the hallway. He pulled down his facemask and they did the same.

'I can't tell you much more than you've already surmised. She was strangled in the bath. There are thumbprints and fingermarks around her aorta, and the splash patterns on the wall are consistent with her arms flailing. Poor woman. The killer was determined it would work first time. There was significant pressure applied from what I can deduce in this setting. I've placed an initial time of death at between 5 and 7 p.m. I'll expect one of you at the post-mortem, which I intend to conduct first thing tomorrow. If you happen to arrest someone do let me know and I'll get in earlier than my planned eight o'clock start. I wish you luck,' King said as he nodded at the officer on the door to the flat to be released.

'Well, that was no help,' Moretti remarked once he was confident King wouldn't return.

'He's a professional man and very good at his job. He wants the killer caught as much as we do. If there was anything else that would assist us, he'd say,' Nash replied as Jonesy entered the flat and stood in the hall.

'What's that?' Nash asked, pointing at the CCTV hard drive that he was holding.

'It's the main CCTV system for the block. Where's Mike? He's the designated exhibits officer, isn't he? I need to book it in with him,' Jonesy said.

'Why don't we just get the techies out and copy it?' Moretti asked him.

than at the base of her neck and back of her head now that hair had been removed. A bruise was evident, indicative of where her head had been bashed against the rim of the roll top bath before being held below the surface of the water against the floor of the tub. There were no signs of recent sexual activity. Bloods had been taken for toxicology and they'd have to wait on those results.

There was an absence of any prescription medications at the scene. Paracetamol was the strongest tablet found. That packet was a blister pack and only two were missing from a new box purchased locally. The sticky price label on the outside told them this. No drug paraphernalia was present or spent works. It's not unknown for wealthy professionals in the city to partake of a line of cocaine – whatever it took to keep these high-flyers awake, productive and ahead of their competition.

Moretti welcomed the fresh air as he exited the mortuary building. He needed to call Nash to update her on the results but he needed a smoke. He'd vowed to Nash before Christmas he'd give up – again. He wasn't one for New Year resolutions. Dry January and Veganuary could take a hike until the same time next year.

He blinked against the sun's harsh rays as he leant against the building's wall. He found his Ray-Bans and put them on. Dr King would have a busy morning as a few of the slabs were already occupied. A triple stabbing from last night had been picked up by one of the other teams.

Moretti's phone vibrated in his trouser pocket. He looked at the screen. The name "Wotnow" was displayed. It was Nash.

'I was about to call you,' he said.

He inhaled on his Savinelli briar one last time as he scanned for a cigarette bin to tap the spent ash out of the bowl. He whacked the bowl against the sole of his boot and floored it into a patch of grass.

'You always say that and yet here I am chasing you for the update the team are all waiting for,' she jested.

He updated Nash on what Dr King had discovered. Nash made noises that told Moretti she was listening. The conversation was brief.

'Come back to the office. I'll meet you there and we'll head out. I need to visit somewhere then we'll go over to the victim's place of work,' Nash informed him.

'Sure. Has the victim's family been told?' he enquired.

'Yes. I had a call from George. They're flying over from Germany today. JJ will meet them at the airport with Frank. He's the FLO for this one. What happened to the cat? The family were asking. And also a pet passport that the victim had for it?' Nash asked.

'I'll call JJ and ask him. I assumed the RSPCA had collected it but I'll confirm with him,' he replied.

Nash hung up and Moretti rang JJ. The phone rang out a while before it was answered. In the background Moretti heard a loud bass beat and the sound of something heavy and metallic being dropped to the floor. He held his phone's speaker away from his ear. The music reduced in volume as JJ's deep voice appeared on the line.

'Skip, what's up?' he asked. His voice clambering for breath.

'Where are you? It sounds like a night club?'

'I'm in the basement gym, quick set for the guns then I'm on it, promise. I missed a day's training yesterday so my head's messed up, but all good now,' JJ replied.

'Be quick. Nash's coming back from wherever she's holed up and she thinks you're all out where you should be. JJ, we do have a live job you know?' Moretti reminded him. The tone of his voice was indicative that he was serious.

JJ remained silent but Moretti could make out from his steadied breathing he felt guilt at his warped priorities.

'Fair enough, Nick, I'm on it. Was there something you needed?' he asked respectfully.

'She was asking about the cat. The RSPCA collected it from the flat, right?'

Moretti waited for JJ's response. There was silence. A silence that every detective knows means the shit's about to hit the fan.

'Shit… shit… shit, I've gotta go.' JJ killed the call.

Moretti stared at his phone. They'd had a busy end to the year and as much as he appreciated they'd be exhausted, he required everyone's full attention to the case. He'd deal directly with JJ regarding the cat, which he was all too aware could be a major issue. Nash's answer could wait. For how long was the only question.

For DC Jules Jackson, or JJ, as he was known to all, the last call he'd taken was going to go down in history as one of his worst. He sat on the weights bench and lay down between the two support brackets under the long bar that loomed above his eyeline. What would have filled him with joy, as he used it to work out his pectoral muscles, now filled him with trepidation. He wanted the gym to cave in and swallow him up.

He covered his face with his calloused shovel hands. Sweat rolled from his close-cropped Afro as he tried to remember what he'd done with that blue crate. The blue crate he'd been extra careful to ensure was secured but comfortable for his adopted feline companion.

He scooped up his job mobile from the floor where he'd thrown it as soon as he'd hung up on Moretti. It was still serviceable thanks to the protective cover it was contained in. Builder proof.

He dispensed with his shower, dressed and went back to the office. As he entered the incident room he let his eyes rove until they latched on to whom he needed. DC Mike Brown the exhibits officer. He nodded at Brown in the internationally recognised way that indicated he needed to step outside and fast. Brown pointed at himself, and when JJ rapidly confirmed with his head it was him that he so desperately required, he got up and strolled outside into a small room that stored the team's filing cabinets.

JJ shut the door. They both stood in the thin corridor between the two banks of cabinets whose drawers were braced at the front by a steel rod and padlocked at the top. JJ leant against one; his hands cupped his chin while his fingers braced his cheeks.

'Mike, I'm in the shit,' he explained.

'Go on,' Brown said, giving JJ time to get composed. He wouldn't give him long as he had a desk of exhibits that needed to go back in the cage. Leaving them in an open office wasn't something he desired. Cops were terrible for pranks.

'The blue crate... the blue crate... where is it?' JJ asked.

'There are loads of blue crates... wait... not the one with the cat in? You prick!'

'Fuck me, Mike, this is serious. I've lost the victim's pet. Nash finds out and I'm off the unit or worse, out of a job for neglect of duty,' JJ said.

Mike realised that JJ may not be the only one to lose his job. Mike was exhibits officer and it was his primary purpose to account for every exhibit from finding to court. He'd have to explain everything that had happened to that cat and should know where it was. All movement needed to come through him. He composed himself and placed both hands on his mate's shoulders.

'Jonesy took a load of crates back last night. It must have been among those. They're in the exhibits cage. I'll get the key and we'll go and find it. You can give me a hand to carry some stuff down there so it won't make it so obvious,' Mike replied.

They entered the room and began to search.

* * *

Nash was back in her office. She'd brought a takeout coffee for herself. Moretti rushed past her open office door saying nothing. She thought he looked flustered and put that down to a new investigation and the pressure that came when a murder broke. The first two weeks usually being the most intense. She sat down and checked her emails. Twenty minutes passed when her attention was interrupted by a shadow cast across her desk. JJ framed the doorway and gave a soft knock.

'It's open, sit down,' she said.

Johnson did as instructed, pushing the door over behind him but not so far that it shut completely. It was as though he was making preparation for a hasty escape. He sat on the makeshift bed Nash had arranged and sat forward, his hands out in front of him, head down. Nash sensed she was about to hear a confession. She'd seen the pose from many detectives when they were about to own up to one or many misdemeanours or sleights of judgement. If it arrived at her door, and not Moretti's, she knew the problem was bigger than the DS wished to manage. Nash dimmed her screen and nodded for JJ to speak.

'Out with it, big man,' she said.

JJ looked up, his pupils like orbs of angst trapped in a milk pond.

'Boss, I've screwed up… really messed up… I was tired from many things: work, life, training and, bottom line, I've lost the crate with the cat in. I dunno where it is. I've turned the exhibits room upside down but I can't find it. I asked Jonesy and he says he never collected it from Mike… Look, I'm not blaming anyone else but me; I'm just saying I don't know where the fuck the thing is.'

JJ turned to look out the window that overlooked the parade square such was his embarrassment.

A knock at the door caused both their heads to snap across at the entrance as Moretti appeared. He eased himself into the room conscious he'd arrived at just the wrong time.

'There you are, JJ…'

'Get in here, now, and get Mike too,' Nash said.

Moretti's head jolted back at the venom in her voice. He shouted for Brown who had been waiting outside and stepped across the Rubicon into Nash's office. They both sat next to JJ.

Nash smoothed her skirt and addressed them all.

'I expect professionalism from my staff at all times. Especially when they are at a murder scene. I shouldn't need to remind experienced detectives that the control of exhibits is paramount.'

None of them budged from their respective positions as she continued.

'A simple task. Call the RSPCA and make sure Melissa's pet is taken care of and yet none of you had the common sense to ensure that was done, and yes, I'm referring to you too, DS Moretti, as I expressly asked you to make sure of this. But no, here we all are, the victim's family arriving all the way from Germany to ID their only daughter and take possession of a significant reminder of their daughter's life, and you three have gone and lost it!'

Nash sat back and let them stew.

They sat in silence. All looked away from Nash. Her desk had become a barrier of authority. Moretti looked at the door and wished he could leave, angry at his admonishment in front of the DCs but in his heart knew it was deserved. JJ looked out the window and wished he was back in the gym, anywhere but here in front of judge and executioner the Right Honourable, Pippa Nash. Brown stared at the floor as he contemplated a life back on a borough CID team or worse, uniform.

Moretti was the first to offer an explanation.

'Look, guv, I just want to expl–'

Nash was rocking from side to side in her swivel chair. She had the appearance of a villain from an old James Bond film. The cat was on her lap. It pawed at her legs until it was in a comfortable position and settled. As she stroked the head of the white ball of fluff, the cat purred with contentment. From where all the offenders sat they couldn't see Nash's feet where the blue crate had been the entire time.

Nash had found the crate last night after hearing scratching coming from within. It had been left in the incident room. A chance discovery but one she was glad to have made. The cat was drowsy, but fine, and she'd given it water and it relaxed. She'd brought food back from the small Tesco Express supermarket next to the cafe she'd visited earlier, along with two bowls, a lead and a litter tray.

The room remained silent as they watched her stroke the feline. Nash's eyes bore into them. She draped the cat over her shoulder as she got up and walked over to where they were sat. She perched on the edge of her desk; her voice became lower and serene in tone but contained the same veracity of message.

'Wake up. All of you, and get on with the job I expect you to do. JJ, take the cat out for the toilet. There's a lead in the carrier by your feet,' she said, then turned to Moretti. 'DS Moretti, go back out there and make sure *everyone* is under no illusion that I will stand for nothing but one hundred percent professionalism and effort in the apprehension of Melissa's killer. Do I make myself clear?'

'Yes,' he replied.

They both got up and Nash handed JJ the cat.

'The victim's family will be at the mortuary at midday. I want the cat to be available to them along with the passport that's in the same bag as the lead. I've phoned the airport and they will ensure the family are met by an airport official who will ensure the cat is placed in a secure crate, in comfort, for travel back to Germany. It's called victim care, something you all need to remind yourselves about.'

Nash turned her back on them. She'd left Frank Mason, the FLO, out of the arrangements. She didn't wish him to be involved with this side of the house, it being such a mess, until she was satisfied she'd made all the arrangements that were needed. Meeting done.

Nash handed Brown four statements of continuity for the care of the cat. One for him, the rest were copies for the inside team. He accepted the statements and they all paraded out in silence. Nash shut her door.

Five minutes later she strode to the window and looked out. Below, on a small grass area, was JJ. The cat was attached to a pink sparkling lead, as he tried in vain to make it walk and toilet. Nash stifled a laugh and struggled to hold her coffee steady at the sight of JJ, as he tried in such a gentle way to coax the moggy to move as it played with the lead and rolled on its back.

She turned back and grabbed her jacket and keys to her car. As she walked across the parade square she smiled and waved in the direction of JJ. He nodded and raised his eyes; relieved his nightmare was over. That was until he realised Nash wasn't the only spectator. JJ turned and looked up. All he saw was a sea of other murder team detectives who stared and nudged each other as they waved at him and laughed at the sight he presented. JJ raised his hands in surrender, scooped up the cat and went back inside.

CHAPTER FOUR

Nash turned up the volume on the car radio as Interpol's *The Weekend* played. She wished it were the weekend and one she wasn't on call for. She also wished she'd said no to DS Harris on the undercover unit when asked to deploy on one of his jobs, especially as she'd just lectured Moretti and the others that everyone must remain focussed on the murder. Nash was a trained undercover officer and had managed to avoid the unit's radar since working on Homicide. A recent piece of joint work had come up where DS Harris needed a driver, and Nash fit the bill.

Nash saw the mobile phone shop she required and parked her car well away from the venue. She'd always used this place when she was active in her undercover role and needed a pay-as-you-go phone for cash, no questions asked.

Neon lights lit up the phone shop's window. An assortment of second-hand phones were arranged in a display, along with an advert for Got Ur Back phone software. This allowed the phone user to track his or her phone with ease should it get stolen; there was no long-term payment or signup required, and it was better than the one installed on the phone at manufacture. An iron grille covered the window. This was a new development since she'd last visited.

Before she entered the phone shop, she took off her jacket and undid a couple of shirt buttons. Dress up to dress down. Plus, she knew the owner was a pervert where she was concerned. He'd told her to call him Mace. A nickname of his and she didn't question it. She hated technology, and at this shop a technically savvy assistant would set the phone up or repair screens if required, at no extra cost. All part of the care package that came with each phone sold.

A buzzer sounded as Nash entered, her Barbour biker's jacket slung over her shoulder as she strode in.

'Well, well, well... long time no see,' the Albanian owner said, the same man Nash knew as Mace. His eyes immediately dropped to her cleavage.

'Business been slow for you then?' he enquired with a wry smile.

'Eyes up, Mace,' she said as she browsed a display of various pay-as-you-go, unlocked phones.

'Don't bother yourself with any of those pieces of shit. As a valued customer I will look in the back for something better for you,' he said.

x

The owner shouted out to the void. A male in his twenties, olive skin, with similar dark sweptback hair as the owner, appeared from a dimly lit side room.

'Go get the good stuff for our beautiful princess here,' Mace said.

The younger man nodded and left.

'Just the phones and a couple of SIM cards will be great. So, what's with the window?' Nash asked the owner and they both glanced at the grille.

The security measure was a robust feature, and as the sun cleared the rooftops of the surrounding buildings, the metal bars cast a cage-like image on the shop's industrial-carpeted floor.

'Those bastards on mopeds robbed me last week. Cleaned me out of everything I had, along with the cash from the till. I have lost good customers, decent people who always drop phones, but know I give best price to fix screen,' Mace said as his assistant came back and left a selection of phones in a box on the counter.

'So, take your pick. All been serviced and I give you a good price for two if one of them is a smartphone…'

Nash picked up the latest iPhone. She placed it down and sifted through various Nokias before she settled on two. The iPhone was one of them, along with a basic Nokia.

'I'll take these if the price is right. I'll need a car charger for both, and a spare battery for the Nokia.'

'Of course, of course, I always look after you,' he said, as he brought a box of SIM cards out from under the counter and a spare battery for the Nokia. Everything was sealed.

They haggled on price. Mace turned the phones on to prove they worked. Once Nash was satisfied the Commissioner was getting value for money, she paid Mace in cash and left.

CHAPTER FIVE

The block's cold atmosphere hadn't changed as Moretti reclined in the concierge's seat and made notes in his decision log, while a couple of detectives canvassed the flats' inhabitants again. It had been a week since the murder, and with very little progress. No leads were surfacing, and Moretti had hoped an anniversary visit to the area would produce someone who may have remembered something of use to the enquiry.

Nash was back at the incident room with the remainder of the team, all of whom were sat around a large meeting table, eager to get any update that would add a positive spin on the investigation. Nash updated them on the progress so far.

'Toxicology has returned a negative hit for any drugs, and witness appeals are proving futile. CCTV from Vauxhall station has captured an image of what appears to be a dispatch rider. He or she is seen entering the block ten minutes before the victim arrived home. The subject's observed to leave thirty minutes after the latest time of death of 7 p.m., given by Dr King.'

Some of the team shifted to a more comfortable position in the hard-backed seats. She continued despite the team's feeling that the job was as stale as a canteen roll.

She tapped the return key on her laptop and the main screen it was linked to displayed the CCTV footage.

'As can be seen, the rider waits for a resident to enter the block and follows him in. Notice our rider's carrying a Jiffy bag. The concierge is nowhere to be seen.' She paused as Jonesy let out a groan.

She continued, 'That's all the coverage provides us with. The man who let the rider in has been spoken to. He confirmed, somewhat embarrassed, that he hadn't realised he'd let the person in, as he was concentrating on a call and didn't take any notice of who was behind him. The rider was then seen to leave the building without the Jiffy envelope,' Nash said.

All eyes were on the screen.

'No Jiffy bag was found at the scene. Enquiries are in hand to see if any other resident had taken a delivery at that time. If that isn't the case, then one possible theory is the rider is our suspect and the Jiffy bag contained the implement used to gain access to the victim's flat. On exiting the building, the bag may have been secreted in their jacket. Bins have been searched with a negative result. They hadn't been collected, so if they'd dumped the scanner or any other device to access her door, it would have been found. Drains close to the block have been lifted and a camera probe sent down just in case. Nothing. I'm liaising with the dive team manager who sent a couple of his officers down there on the night to see if it's worth another visit.' Nash stopped the CCTV footage.

DC Colette Booth continued after getting the nod from Nash. 'Witness appeals have been updated with the anniversary plea: witness boards, all social media platforms in addition to TV and local press. A CCTV image of the rider has been released on your authority, ma'am, as a person of interest we wish to trace and eliminate from the investigation. As we can see, there's not much to go on with the rider – all dark clothing, no bike seen nearby or any company logo to work off. The footage has been enhanced and the dark shadow is a balaclava that was worn. It covered the mouth and nose. From the image it wasn't possible to accurately determine ethnicity or sex. A boot impression has been lifted from the bathroom floor. The pink from the bath bomb stained it and revealed a pattern from the sole. That find hasn't been made public, again at your request, boss.'

Jonesy spoke up.

'I visited the victim's place of work and spoke to all members of staff there. It's a bespoke firm with a small team of five. They deal with high-end clients' advertising needs. The victim was a much-loved team member. A person dedicated to her job. She'd been there from the off and grafted her way to the position of CEO. She wasn't in any current relationship as far as they knew. Work was her passion. She'd been in relationships up until a year ago when the last one ended. It had been a thing of some six months and they'd parted under a mutual understanding that they weren't compatible.'

Jonesy paused to check his notes then continued.

'I contacted the victim's ex and visited her with DS Moretti. She was shocked to hear the news and was naturally upset. DS Moretti and I were satisfied that the ex was genuine in her responses to questions we asked. She'd provided an alibi for her movements along with a theatre ticket stub. She was at The Garrick at the time Melissa would've been murdered. Enquiries at The Garrick corroborated the account by way of the theatre's CCTV and ticket. Staff had the name as she'd collected her ticket on the day,' Jonesy said as he closed his daybook and sat back.

Nash cradled her pen like a drummer palms their sticks while she tapped her decision log slowly as she thought. It was an annoying trait of hers but the team now knew they'd be departing soon, as this was a pattern she performed before wrapping any meeting up.

Nash stopped her drum solo and looked up at Sagona. 'George, I want a meeting later re any outstanding actions.'

He nodded at Nash as he dispersed crumbs from his belly. Nash continued and addressed DS Owen Matthews from the Intel desk.

'Owen, I need an up-to-date list of all dispatch firms within a mile's radius of the victim's block and work. We'll start there and expand parameters if required. I also want the victim's phone records for the last month – both work and personal. Any problems with the work side then let me know. Finally, I need details of any social media accounts she may have used. Everyone else, see George. Get any actions from him. I want them turned around quickly please and the system updated by your phones while you're out. Any other business?' Nash scanned the room and everyone shook their heads.

'That's all.' She closed the briefing and shut the lid to her laptop. Chairs scraped back and the room dispersed, leaving the electrical fizz of the overhead projector as the last trace of the room's occupation.

CHAPTER SIX

Nash knocked on the door to the undercover unit. Behind it she heard a male clearing his throat and the plain brown fire door opened. A gruff sounding DS, Carl Harris, stood before her. His planet-sized fist covered his mouth while he motioned her in with his free hand, and kicked the door closed behind them. A pointless act, as the restraining mechanism slowed the momentum to a crawl. Harris was wearing a short sleeve white shirt and dark blue jeans. The shirt hugged his torso as it was designed to. Nash felt good to be back in the world she loved. This also justified her reason for never being on camera for witness appeals or updates outside court, much to her Detective Chief Inspector's chagrin.

Harris motioned for Nash to grab the spare seat. A seat which had seen better days but was still fit for purpose – just.

'How's tricks, Pip?' Harris enquired as he sat across from her and shuffled through papers on his desk until he found the folder he sought.

'All good aside from the business end of murder being on the up,' she replied, taking out her phones and placing them on the table.

Harris looked down at the three that sat there and then back up at Nash and raised his eyebrows. She smiled and took each phone's battery out and made an exaggerated show of displaying that the iPhone was off.

'I thought you'd have the phone cages installed by now. The National Crime Agency have them, as do the Confidential Intelligence Unit…' Nash let that hang.

Harris could see the wry smirk accented on her jaw and waved his index finger at her.

'I'm not taking the bait, my friend. We are more than happy to save the Commissioner's money and have any visitors break up their phones and leave them on display. Now, to business.'

'No coffees? Another budget saving scheme you've introduced? Anyone would think you're after a promotion,' Nash quipped, as she hesitantly leaned back in the chair to test its strength.

Harris sat forward and opened up the file. Banter over, it was down to business.

'So, I need you to introduce someone to me. I've been working with the Economic Crime Unit and we've set up a nice little sting. It's working a treat, but not attracting the right people.'

'Go on,' she said, with a degree of hesitation as she racked her brain as to how she could be of any use or know someone Harris would need introducing to.

Harris continued.

'We've set up a sting shop in Kings Cross. It's a small unit that purports to take in second-hand goods for sale. So far we've had it running for a month and let's say the trade has been a tad steady. Word's getting out and we've had a few takers who've asked the right questions and got the right reply but the gear that's coming over the counter isn't phones and that's our target market.' Harris paused and flicked through a few A4 sheets in the file. 'I'm not after a few junkies looking to sell their mum's nicked rings. As sad as that is, that's not going to help this operation continue.'

'So where do I fit in? I haven't got the capacity for anything long-term, Carl, so I'm not going on any rota for errand girl or front of house totty,' Nash said, raising an eyebrow.

'As if I would use your excellent female guile and detective ability for such a menial task,' Harris said. 'Right, where were we…'

Harris slid a printed colour image across to her. The image had been taken by a surveillance team and showed a male's face. The male was standing outside a house. The face was turned to the camera; a face Nash knew all too well.

She picked up the print and bit her bottom lip. Harris sat back and returned his arms behind his head. As Nash glanced up, Harris grinned and started to laugh.

'Who'd have thought all my luck would fall into place so quickly?' Harris slid another image over that showed Nash exiting her favourite phone shop. 'All said, you picked a great place to get your burner phones. Good skills. Now, obviously our mutual associate doesn't know you're Old Bill?'

Nash gave a wry smile. 'So, what do you need me to do and how the hell has he come into your enquiry?' she asked.

Harris pushed the remainder of the file that had contained the photographs towards her.

'Read this for background but you can't take it away. The shop you visit is taking in nicked phones from smash and grabs and sending them abroad. Not just the odd one, but enough to justify the use of a corner of a shipping container. A large corner, mind you. I need you to introduce your man to me. I'm aware I could just wander in myself but I'm getting pressure from above for results and with what I have in mind you could help me achieve them far quicker,' Harris said.

Nash looked through the file.

'I'm not entirely convinced you're right about this one. When I was there the other day, the windows were boarded up after they'd been put through and his stock stolen. He told me it was the smash and grab lot that robbed his place,' Nash said.

Harris rocked from side to side in his office chair as he contemplated his reply.

'The robbery was staged,' he said.

'Staged?'

'In the file is what analysts call an association chart. To you and me, it's a pretty diagram that shows the shop owner's associates, phone numbers and premises. They all link up and correlate a connection with his shop. He's running these moped gangs and they're stealing to order. The phones are getting forensically wiped, restored and shipped back to Albania for resale and onward distribution. The money we're talking about here is staggering. Millions of pounds being made off the back of these robberies.'

Harris got up and walked to a kettle. He placed a heaped scoop of instant into two Styrofoam cups and shook the kettle. Satisfied it contained enough water, he flicked it on and waited for it to boil while he checked his own phone for any messages.

Nash took out the association chart and had a look. Various sheets had been taped together and she draped these out on the desk. At first glance it contained multiple linking lines, spidering out from the phone shop in the centre of the sheets to other graphics of telephones, cars and residential and business premises. One premises was a shipping container company. She could see that a lot of effort had gone into the job already. The kettle clicked and Harris poured out the boiled water and returned to the desk with the drinks.

'That's not all our work.' Harris nodded at the chart. 'Our job has crossed over with another. I wouldn't see you having any further involvement beyond the introduction of my good self,' he said then took a sip of coffee.

'How do you propose I introduce you?' she asked.

'All I'd like you to do is bring me to the shop as a place that would be good for me to buy my phones from. After you make the introduction, you leave and that's it. My hope is that with you as a reference point the owner will relax and I can have a chat with him. The ins and outs of that you don't need to know,' Harris said as he scratched his chest.

'When do you want to do this? I've a live murder investigation at the moment.'

'Well, with the best will in the world I've seen the news and it's hardly alive… I thought we could strike while the iron's hot and go within the hour?' Harris said.

Nash shook her head at the brazen gall. She started to read through the file again. She switched her work phone back on and there was a text from Moretti to call her; not urgent.

'I'll go and get the DI from the operational team. She's in the canteen and we'll run through the usual *use and conduct* stuff then once you're signed off, we'll go. I took the liberty of getting your paperwork up and running as I knew you couldn't refuse coming back for some fun,' Harris said.

'Fine,' Nash replied as she continued to read more of the paperwork and profiles it contained.

Harris got up and patted her on the shoulder as he passed her.

'You may want to leave the phones that you bought with me. I have a couple of others you can have.'

With that, Harris left Nash to her reading while he went to find the operational team's DI.

CHAPTER SEVEN

Nash waited by Angel tube station for Moretti to pick her up. Not the best of places for him to pull over but a place he knew well, so they'd agreed on that. Nash had completed her role with Harris and had introduced him to Mace as he'd asked. It had all gone smoothly. Mace was relieved there wasn't an issue with the phones he'd sold her. Nash had laughed when she left. Mace had looked as though she'd brought along her enforcer and was overjoyed when that wasn't the case. Nash looked up from where she was sitting and saw Moretti crawling along in traffic. She waved, grabbed her belongings and ventured into the road. As the car stopped at traffic lights, Moretti released the door lock and she jumped in.

'All go OK in the world of talking out the corner of your mouth and wearing overpriced suits?' he said as Nash drew the seatbelt across her and into the holder.

'Need to know basis,' she replied, with a smile and her tongue in her cheek.

Moretti rolled his eyes, the lights changed, and he drove towards Holborn.

'Any updates from the enquiry?' Nash asked.

'That's why I texted you. Melissa's parents want to see you. They're staying at a hotel in Holborn, so they agreed to meet us there before they leave to collect Melissa's property. I said I'd bring it to them or get the FLO to, but they'd rather collect it. It will help them with closure, they said. Make the unbelievable real.'

They crossed the lights at Mount Pleasant and headed towards the city.

They reached the hotel, Moretti parked up and they walked to the entrance. The hotel's receptionist greeted them and they were motioned into a bar area where a couple stared out of the window. The female of the couple looked up at them. Her eyes red and face pale. It was as though an older version of Melissa stared back at Nash and Moretti. The woman tapped the male who sat next to her on the arm. He looked away from where his gaze had been locked.

'Mr and Mrs Phelps?'

They both nodded at Moretti.

'We spoke on the phone, Mrs Phelps. I'm DS Nick Moretti and this is DI Pippa Nash. May we sit down?'

There was a moment's pause before Mrs Phelps replied.

'Yes, yes… of course, please do,' she said, as she motioned with her hand for them to take the seats opposite them.

A waitress from the bar approached and asked if they wanted tea or coffee and they all declined. The bar area was empty and Nash waited for the waitress to leave before she spoke.

'I'm very sorry for your loss. Are you happy to speak here? I can ask if there's a private room should you rather that?' Nash said as she looked between them both.

Mrs Phelps let out a sigh and shook her head. Mr Phelps remained impassive. He took a deep swallow and mirrored his wife's response.

Nash continued, 'I have some questions that I need to ask if you'd be good enough to answer them.'

Nash adjusted her seating position, her legs side-on to them both, hands in her lap as she leaned forward.

'When you last spoke to Melissa, did she mention anything or anyone that had been troubling her?' Nash said.

Mrs Phelps looked at her husband who sat with a thousand-yard stare. She touched his hand and stroked the back of it then answered Nash's question.

'I spoke with Melissa a week ago. She sounded happy with life and never expressed any concern. As her mother, I've always known if there was anything troubling her. I could tell in her voice, you see. We were very close, all three of us. There was nothing she said that gave me any cause for concern, but no one could predict what has happened, Inspector, surely?'

Nash nodded. 'Absolutely. I'm just trying to get an idea of your daughter's likes, dislikes, friends, relationships, anything that could give us an opening as to who would wish her to come to such harm,' Nash said, and waited as Mrs Phelps took out a hanky and ruffled it in her spare hand.

'Inspector, we've come here to collect what's left of our daughter's life and to arrange for her to come home to be laid to rest. There's nothing we can tell you that will help find the bastard who killed her... I'm sorry... I only wish there was.' Mrs Phelps gripped her husband's hand and both Nash and Moretti could see the tears that began to surface in both parents' eyes.

Moretti had informed the manager they were to be left alone for the next twenty minutes, and the manager was astute enough to not ask questions. She'd seen the papers and recognised the surname when the Phelpses had been booked in. She assured Moretti of complete privacy.

Moretti gave a warm smile to Mrs Phelps. 'I'm so sorry you have to go through this but we shouldn't be too much longer. You're right, there may not be anything you consider important but sometimes the smallest detail that may appear irrelevant can provide a breakthrough for an investigative team,' he said.

Mrs Phelps returned his warmth and nodded her head in acknowledgement at his genuine empathy. She turned to Nash.

'You know, you remind me of Melissa: warm, kind and sincere. I'll miss talking with her. We would talk every week… sometimes it would be using WhatsApp or Messenger or Facebook and she loved Instagram. I'll miss seeing her photos, she takes such lovely photos… took such lovely photos… oh dear.' Mrs Phelps collapsed into her husband's side and sobbed.

He remained perfectly still then slowly placed his arm around her shoulders and looked directly at Nash.

'Find the bastard who killed my daughter and when you do, make sure they don't come quietly. With any luck they'll live at the top of a tower block where the lift is broken and take an unexpected fall down many flights of stairs. Now, I'd like some time with my wife before the other officer arrives. If there's anything else you need then obviously we'll do our best to help. We always do our best to help anyone and Melissa was the same, such a sweet loving person.'

He finished speaking, turned and kissed his wife on the side of her head that was buried into his shoulder and whose tears gradually soaked his blue Oxford shirt. Nash nodded at Moretti and they both got up. Nash passed Mr Phelps a card.

'If you need anything then call me. My mobile is always on should you think of anything while you are here. My team will do all they can to bring the perpetrator to justice,' she said before she and Moretti left them alone on the small two-seat Chesterfield sofa to experience their grief.

As Nash closed the door to the bar she looked back at the couple and took a deep breath. She could feel a pain in her stomach and hoped she'd have closure for them soon.

CHAPTER EIGHT

The briefing room fell silent as Nash joined her team. Moretti sat at his usual place alongside Nash at the head of the table. Nash opened her daybook and glanced around. All were present who were expected to be there. She updated the team on the meeting with Melissa's parents and turned to the Intelligence Desk manager, DS Owen Matthews.

'Owen, in addition to the social media accounts, I need a breakdown to differentiate between friends and family and provide me with some knowledge about any groups she belonged to or any areas of interest she highlighted. We're at an impasse as far as intelligence is concerned, and all we've discovered about her hasn't provided a lead, suspect, or any possible motive for her murder. No forced entry to the flat bothers me. She either let the person in because she knew them or the lock was bypassed electronically. I've asked for the lock to be removed and forensically examined to see if there's any indication it's been hacked. I want her phone records and emails checked for any deliveries on the day she was murdered: food, drink, shopping, anything.'

DS Matthews nodded and scribbled down the tasking.

Nash turned to the source unit DS, Hugo Dillon, who'd agreed to attend at her request. 'Anything from your sources?'

'Nothing as yet. We've shown the image of the dispatch rider to a few of our friendlies and they've all drawn a blank. We'll keep up the pressure for information and if one of them hears anything then they'll be in touch, that's for certain,' Dillon said.

Nash continued, 'Anyone else got any new information for the table? I need some answers, people. This poor woman came home to be strangled in her bath and all we have is a grainy image of a dispatch rider that may or may not have any bearing on the investigation.'

Nash's work phone vibrated in her pocket. She looked at the screen and saw it was the contact desk. She excused herself from the room and stepped out to take the call.

'DI Nash?' a voice asked.

'Yes, how can I help you?'

'Ma'am, I've an officer on scene of a suspicious death. He's requested that you be contacted as his team attended one similar to where they are now and—'

'Sorry, are you saying the officer attended the scene at flat 33, Thamesmere Heights, and the circumstances are similar?'

'Yes. I've accessed the restricted Computer Aided Dispatch report for the previous incident and compared the two. They would appear identical. Obviously, I'm not linking anything until a homicide detective has made an assessment,' the contact desk officer said.

'Pass the details to DS Moretti and myself. I will have the scene looked at and a decision made if it's for us.' Nash hung up.

She drew her fingers over her ponytail and rubbed her mouth before she re-entered the briefing room. The voices that had been circulating quietened as all eyes fell on her. They all knew the look of a DI who'd been given a new job. Heads dropped while others clasped their faces and peered through fingers at her.

She leaned on the desk. 'Not confirmed, but we may have another job identical to the Phelps murder. Nick, go down to this new scene. Make an assessment as to whether this is linked, or not, based on the MO. Until I get feedback from DS Moretti, we all carry on with our current duties. No one is to book off or go home until they've spoken to me, understood?'

All heads nodded and the meeting was brought to a close.

Nash lightly grabbed Moretti's arm as he was about to leave. Once the room was clear she spoke quietly. 'It appears identical from what I've been told on the phone but make your own assessment and feedback to me. I know you're interested in taking the exam for inspector so this will all add to your application,' she told him then added, 'but more importantly, I trust your judgement. Any doubts, let me know and I will be straight down.'

Moretti gathered up his daybook and on his way out, shouted for Jonesy to grab his scene bag as well as his own and to meet him in the parade square.

CHAPTER NINE

Moretti waited outside what appeared to be a newly decorated bathroom. The ivory grout was flush with the tiles, pristine and untouched by water damage. The latest victim lay face up in the water as though she'd fallen asleep, but he knew that wasn't the case. He let his eyes take in the room as they searched.

The detectives detailed with the scene examination all moved from the ceiling down as they scrutinised every available space for anything that stood out as unusual or out of place. All searched for a clue that could lead to an investigative breakthrough. If it belonged in the flat, why was it where it was when it could have been situated elsewhere? The very question Moretti asked himself of Jade Williams, the bath's occupant.

Dr King leant over the lifeless body while he moved a strand of long lank Afro curl from Jade's forehead. The bath's tap emitted a steady drip, the echo of which had become an irritant to those alive in the small space. It felt like déjà vu to Moretti. Nash had joined them once Moretti had got the ball rolling. As soon as he'd seen the body, he'd placed a call to her.

There were no signs of forced entry to the flat. It was situated two blocks along the river towards Battersea power station from where Melissa had resided and incorporated the same entry system.

JJ and Jonesy were absorbed in the search of the flat with DC Katriona 'Katie' Maloney, the designated exhibits officer for this case. Yvonne Campbell, the SOCO, was studiously dusting a single wardrobe's interior in the main bedroom. The doors of which had been open when the first officers arrived and checked for any other occupants. They'd been skilled enough to choose a common approach path and used their body-worn cameras as a visual aid for Moretti to view on his arrival.

This was invaluable for Moretti as he could view footage from the officer's camera without having to enter. The footage where the victim lay was too brief, so he'd taken the decision to enter and assess. He used the same route as the uniform officer had, so the scene remained as undisturbed as possible.

There was a hush to the premises, the peace of which was shattered every so often by the sounds of investigation: the uniform officer's personal radio, and the sound from the photographer's camera flash as it rose from a mute to a crescendo before finally getting released by the shutter button. All officers and support staff were deep in concentration. Every victim mattered. Nash insisted on the ethos at any scene her team attended, and she was honoured to witness it in abundance in each room her staff occupied.

The flat was neat and ordered much like Jade's life appeared to be. She was a barrister for a prominent legal firm. Her office had been visited and the head of chambers informed. He'd struggled to comprehend what he was being told. He explained how valued she was and that he'd just taken a call from the Old Bailey where she'd been due in court and not been seen. A graduation photo sat in a wooden frame perched atop a windowsill in her living room. She was with an older couple that Nash assumed to be her parents as there was a likeness in the eyes.

Pictures attached by magnets clung to the fridge that depicted fun times in Jamaica. The national flag flew above the beach bar they were photographed at. People dressed in flowing white linen, all smiling and relaxed. A far cry from where she lay now surrounded by murky water and a montage of white forensic suits. Dr King stood up. Nash and Moretti moved aside and gave him room to leave the bathroom. They all resumed in the small hall.

Dr King kept his mask on as he spoke, the material moving in and out with every word. 'The MO is identical to the Melissa Phelps murder. Asphyxiation due to strangulation. I will be taking measurements of the bruising again at the mortuary and a comparison will be made of the two cases. I'm confident I'm right, but need a thorough forensic comparison made beyond my cursory observation. Any progress on the Phelps case? I confess I've been so busy I've barely had time to catch up on current affairs,' he said.

'We're no further forward beyond a possible suspect seen on CCTV. It's circumstantial at best. Until we've traced and spoken to the individual then we've made as much progress as a drugged slug.' Nash sighed.

Dr King patted her arm in an unusually fatherly gesture.

'I'll see one of you at 8 a.m. sharp tomorrow for the post mortem. Oh, and Ms Williams was killed between five and seven o'clock last night,' he said as he signed a uniform officer's crime scene log and left.

As they moved back into the living room, they saw JJ. He was coming out of the kitchen carrying a cat basket and shaking his head. 'What is it with high-flyers and pet cats? Like they'd have any time for them being out at work all day? It just ain't fair,' he said, by way of reassurance to an almost identical-looking cat to that of Melissa Phelps's.

A white and brown-flecked cat purred from the wicker cat basket JJ cradled under his pronounced bicep.

Nash looked closer at the entrance to the basket. 'JJ, was the cat in the basket when you found it, and was the door to the basket open or closed?' she asked.

JJ smiled back at her and started shaking his head as he wagged his spare index finger.

'You know, boss, I may not be the best at pet-sitting, but I do know my job. It was shut and locked with the cat in it. I got Yvonne to dust the basket's door as best she could. She's swabbed it for good measure too in case our suspect got a scratch. There's nothing obvious but you never know. Oh, and for your information this ain't the basket from the kitchen either,' JJ said as he continued to nod his head in self-recognition at his sterling work.

'When I took Melissa's cat, I was given this basket as a spare to carry in the car should I ever be in the same situation again. In truth I think, Veronique, the cat shelter supervisor, likes me. She'd intimated that it would be nice to see me again. Looks like it's her lucky day, eh?'

Nash shook her head and smiled. 'Good work, JJ. You're a thinker and if I came across as doubting your abilities then that was never my intention. You know me, I think out loud at times when I should keep quiet. After all, my job's to question. I need to see the others and see where we're all at before Jade's body's removed,' Nash said.

Nash left Moretti speaking with JJ and found Campbell. She'd moved from the wardrobe and was looking at a drinking glass on a bedside table. She dusted down the outside of the glass, the light from the bedroom window creating a shower of colour as she flicked the brush hairs across the surface. She looked up and let the varifocal lens do its job; as her eyes zoned in on the areas, she was keen to explore for any prints. Prints that wouldn't be attributed to Jade. She felt like an artist as she worked, and held the tumbler away from her face to study the glass.

'You never know, our suspect may have taken a moment to have a drink before they left. There's no lipstick mark on it from what I can see, and Jade is wearing lipstick,' she offered, by way of explanation that Nash didn't require, as she could see it for herself but nevertheless respected.

'Stranger things have happened, I'll give you that,' Nash replied.

She liked the way Campbell worked and she'd managed her last case very well, so she was pleased every time she arrived at one of her scenes. Campbell was a methodical worker, much like herself, and she had a lot of time for colleagues who took pride in what they did.

Jonesy drifted in from a spare bedroom and raised his chin at Nash. Nash went to him. Jonesy booked in a laptop he'd found, and two mobile phones with DC Maloney. One smartphone and a Nokia that looked old and beyond working.

'Anything else from that room, Jonesy?' Nash asked.

'That's it,' he said.

There was a knock at the flat's door. Nash turned and saw that the undertakers had arrived to transport Jade to the mortuary. Her team had almost completed all they could do at the flat for today. Nash sat at a small table and looked through what exhibits had been gathered while Jade's body was removed. She'd thought the investigation at the end of last year was her "big" case but now, as she moved the various plastic exhibit bags to the floor, she realised she couldn't have been further from the truth.

CHAPTER TEN

Nash had instructed Moretti to attend Jade's post mortem on the understanding she would deal with the team's actions and updates from yesterday's scene. She'd not slept well. She never did as a matter of rule but when a new murder broke the insomnia became worse. Her mind became the major incident room with no one to turn out the lights at the end of the day. She had two deaths to manage and that meant her mind was in overdrive. She longed for the freedom of a run.

The incident room was alive with the sound of computer keyboards, various discussions and the drinking of coffee. As the room settled, she nodded to Jonesy who activated a roller blind she'd had installed on a portable board. Jonesy turned in his chair and pulled the ring down, letting the mechanism roll the plain white blind upwards. Behind it, Nash had added the picture of Jade Williams along with that of Melissa Phelps. The team had been reluctant to take a step back in time to use the board. HOLMES, the computerised record of everything that was taking place, took care of everything the board, carousel turntable and index cards used to. Nash believed people operated better when they could see the person they worked for. It didn't correlate to bosses but worked for victims. Every member of the team was now the victim's voice. Something a computer couldn't be.

On this occasion she'd decided to use the images obtained from Dr King alongside the images of the victims taken from their homes. Nash hoped King's further exploratory work in the mortuary would corroborate his opinion of a linked case.

Nash sipped her lukewarm coffee and started the meeting.

'DS Moretti is at the post mortem. He'll feedback the results later. In the meantime, let's start with the Jade Williams investigation, then we can look at the Melissa Phelps case…'

'So we are linking the two then?' Sagona asked.

'Not officially – no. I want them to run side by side though. I don't want to miss any similarities… you know the drill.'

As Nash finished speaking, Sagona rolled his eyes.

'George, do not give me that look again. I *never* issue a directive without giving the subject due diligence and I thought you of all people would have realised that by now,' Nash said.

Others in the room adjusted their positions to ones that projected attention. Nash continued. Her team's body language noted.

'Until I get confirmation from Dr King as to the MO, this is how each investigation will run – side by side. King thinks there's a link between the two deaths and given his track record in the field of forensic pathology I wouldn't disagree with him. Especially having witnessed each scene. So, to CCTV, anything from Jade's block?' Nash directed the question at Jonesy.

'Too early to say but from what's been viewed so far there's nothing startling. Same phone entry system as Melissa's block. Usual stream of regulars each day. We've requested footage a week before the death and we're working back from that. On the day, there was a brief power outage that disrupted the system as the backup generator was installed for heat and light only. The CCTV system wasn't on the circuit. I'm in contact with London electricity board to look at the outside connections for any signs of foul play. It was off for twenty minutes then came back on,' he replied.

'House-to-house is still on-going, and a press statement has been released by DCI Carlson. Next of kin has been informed and the FLO is with them,' Nash said and finished writing in her daybook as she looked up.

'Now, where are we with tracing the rider from the Phelps case?' she enquired of DS Matthews.

Matthews smoothed out a page in his decision log. 'We've drawn a blank with local firms. I went through the correspondence from Melissa's flat and among some of it was a poor-looking excuse for a business card from a handyman. My Intel desk did some work on it. When I called you last night on an unrelated matter, you'd mentioned that Williams's bathroom looked to be freshly tiled or at least grouted. I looked at the scene photos for Melissa's flat and the bathroom looks like that's had some work done too.' Matthews paused as he turned the pages back and forth in his book.

'Where's this leading, Owen?' Sagona chipped in.

'I'll tell you where it's leading, Mighty Mouth, if you'd be so kind as to give me the opportunity to present what we've discovered,' Matthews said.

'It would appear that a man giving the name of Neil Buchanan was offering his services in the area as a handyman. He has a website. One of the pictures shows him on a motorbike. I thought he may do jobs that require enough tools to carry in panniers and he could be our mystery dispatch rider. Why he hasn't seen the appeals and isn't coming forward is another matter. We can ask him when we find him.' Matthews closed his book and sat back.

Nash knew it was a lead they'd have to follow up on. It was a reasonable line of enquiry and if Buchanan had access to the flats in order to work, they'd need to know. He may even have been given access to the app that unlocked Melissa's door.

'Do we know where he lives?' Nash asked Matthews.

'There's nothing apparent on searching the name on the card. He has a photo of him on a motorbike and he's looking back into the camera. The index number's displayed. We have an address for a registered keeper, but it isn't the same details given on the business card. It's a start though.'

'Let's speak to this Mr Buchanan and see what he has to say. Treat him as a potential witness but up the game if he doesn't want to play,' Nash replied.

'If there's no other business let's crack on. Owen, I'll come with you to Buchanan's potential address. Bring two DCs,' Nash said.

Owen nodded.

CHAPTER ELEVEN

Nash sat in a non-descript car and observed the outside of the block of flats where the registered keeper of the motorbike was purported to reside. The block stood among other similar drab-looking buildings, all pebbledash and decay, which the council had the temerity to describe as a thriving community estate in the heart of North London. It thrived on poverty, drugs and despondency. A play area gave the allusion that children lived there and could have fun. DS Matthews sat with a half-eaten apple. The other two detectives had utilised a different car.

'Which flat does the registered keeper live in?' Nash asked.

'Third floor, 5C, didn't you listen to the briefing?' Matthews replied sarcastically as he wiped a misted side window.

His nose rose towards his eyes as his pupils reacted to the low sun. He placed his hand that held the almost spent apple against his forehead in salute. The shield helped his vision as he glanced up at the front door to 5C. He'd ensured they were parked a sufficient distance away so as not to alert Buchanan should he appear at a window or on the balcony.

Nash insisted on caution as Buchanan was the only lead they had.

Nash's phone pinged. A WhatsApp message appeared on her phone's screen. The other DCs confirmed they were in position at the back of the building. She let them know by return of message that she and Matthews were going to try the front door.

'Let's go,' Nash said as Matthews searched for somewhere to dump his apple core and opened the glovebox.

'Seriously?' Nash said.

'What? I'll sort it out back at the base,' Matthews replied as they stepped out of the car and made towards the block.

The main entrance was unlocked and the lift wasn't working. Matthews bounded up the stairs two at a time, while Nash took each one with purpose. She felt fit and composed. Preservation of energy was her main focus should Buchanan decide to kick off at the sight of them. She hoped it wouldn't come to that. At the top of the stairs they linked up again and crept towards the main door to the flat. A smell of cooking was emanating from inside. A radio pumped out a steady bass beat. A small window was ajar that overlooked the balcony. Nash assumed it was one to the kitchen.

Nash looked at Matthews and gave him a nod. Matthews knocked on the front door. There was no reply. The music maintained its volume. He tried again, this time with purpose. Still nothing. Matthews lifted the flap to the letterbox that sat halfway up the door. Although the interior of the flap was occupied by bristles he felt a distinctive rush of air. The sensation was soon followed by the bellow of 'Stop Police' being shouted from the rear of the block.

'Fuck, he's bailed out the window at the back!' Matthews yelled into the void.

Nash had reacted to the shouts and was already close to the ground floor. She fled out the rear door. Ahead of her she saw the outline of DC Andy Parker's back. Parker was more of a wrestler than a runner and Nash already knew his lead on the suspect was lost. She caught up with Parker who was doubled over, hands on his knees. Parker jabbed his index finger in the direction of where the runner had now disappeared from view. He'd lost him.

The other DC, Mohammed Begum, was nowhere to be seen until a car shot past them both as he headed in the direction the subject was last seen running. It was no use. The area was like a maze.

'Was it Buchanan?' Nash demanded as Parker caught his breath and began to pat his jacket as though he'd lost his warrant card in the chase.

He produced an asthma inhaler and took a deep lungful. Nash knew it was a waste of time. Parker was fit for nothing. Matthews had now joined them. He too reacted with venom once he'd ascertained the situation.

'Parker! How could you lose him? He was three floors up for fuck's sake! He couldn't just drop and run! Where were you two? Oh no… you were both in the car, weren't you? Neither of you were out of the vehicle where you should've been! He just descended the drain pole like Incy Wincy fucking Spider and was on his toes pissing himself laughing, I bet!'

Nash let Matthews run with it. Matthews was their DS and as far as she was concerned was handling the situation accordingly. Begum would also be getting an earful on his return and it wouldn't just be from Matthews. The team would be livid. Nash's stoic silence was enough for Parker to realise just how pissed off she was. Nash turned to

Parker who was now standing upright. His breathing was now under control.

'Both of you should've been out of the vehicle, not sat in the warmth where you lost the bet to run should Buchanan decamp. Get your car back. You and Begum can go and check who else is in there. The tenant on the books is a female and I don't suppose it was a female who made off?' Nash said.

Parker shook his head.

'Knock on doors in the building. Let any occupant know we wish to speak to anyone who has knowledge of the occupants of 5C. Find out all you can. I need it confirmed that it was Buchanan, but I need whoever it was who ran to feel safe enough to return once the heat's died down. Don't tell the neighbours why we need to see the occupant. Keep it simple and he may return,' Nash said.

Parker nodded.

'Sorry, both of you. We just didn't think anyone would come out of a flat three floors up and it was… well… pointless us both being out the back,' he said.

Matthews raised his eyebrows while he gripped his hair in both hands. He too had to control his breathing but for entirely different reasons. Matthews faced Parker close enough to be considered an invasion of personal space.

'Your job was to cover the back. Not think about it, or debate it.' Matthews shook his head and joined Nash who was already walking towards the front of the building and back to their car.

He'd ensure all could be done to locate Buchanan. He was hopeful he could establish an observation point and had the ideal pair of DCs in mind to provide twenty-four-hour cover on split twelve-hour shifts. Matthews left her to join Parker and Begum.

Nash had taken a call from Moretti on the way back to the Peel Centre base and he'd updated her on the post mortem. It was as they'd suspected, an identical MO. Nash updated him on her morning's work and there'd been a long pause that wasn't due to a loss of signal. She'd see him back at the incident room after she'd spoken with the source unit.

Nash had used the drive back to the incident room to compose herself and calm down after the fiasco she'd witnessed. She parked her car on the parade square as it wasn't in use and entered the main building. Nash knocked on the door to the source unit and waited as the squeak of a chair and the roll of wheels became louder. The door opened and the Silverfox greeted her sat upon his wheeled office chair. He had a mobile phone held to one ear. He raised an index finger and mouthed, 'one minute.'

Nash entered and found a seat. The environment of the covert unit could only be described as stark. Desks were tidy and clear of paper. A fish tank containing a shoal of guppies sat upon a deep window ledge. It provided a calming effect.

The Silverfox finished his conversation and put the mobile down on his desk. The covert officer was known as the Silverfox due to his greying hair and slick looks. He was also as cunning as they came when dealing with sources. He had a unique working partnership with his DS, Hugo Dillon. They belonged to the Metropolitan Police, MO3 – Covert Policing Command. Nash valued the unit as they provided vital support to her investigations and she hoped they would give her job a leg-up now.

'Who was that then?' Nash asked, knowing full well what the answer would be.

'Very good, Pip, very good. Like I would ever tell you…'

They laughed. The Silverfox got up to make them coffee, which Nash desperately needed even if it was at risk of drinking it from the unwashed mugs the unit's detectives drank from.

'Actually, I can let you know about that call, as it goes,' the Silverfox said as he went to the kettle.

'Oh yeah?'

'Have your lot just been on the Warburton Estate looking for a fella?'

'How on earth would one of your sources know that?'

'We have our ways, we have our ways,' the Silverfox replied, as he dumped a spoon of sugar and what looked like powdered milk into each mug.

He added the boiled water and brought the drinks over. He handed Nash hers before he sat down.

'We've hawked that CCTV image from the block and there's been no takers at all. To be fair to them though, it is shit. However, I spoke to George this morning who'd said you were going out on an enquiry. He gave me some of the lowdown on the person you sought. I put a call in to a very good source of mine on the estate you were on. Upshot is they said you shouldn't have put Puff Daddy and Slow Mo on the rear of the block.' He spat out his coffee as he laughed at his own joke and Nash joined him.

It had been a dismal morning and the atmosphere felt colder than the forensics freezer.

'It was Matthews who tipped you off, wasn't it?' she asked with a smile, as she stared at the ceiling and a covered strip light that contained a graveyard for insects.

The Silverfox nodded in confirmation and placed his mug down as his shoulders juddered so much he couldn't hold it well enough without spilling the contents.

'Wait until you make DS or DI, then you'll realise the job's not that simple when you have to manage people and use what resources are available,' Nash said as the Silverfox regained his composure.

'Fair enough, Pip. I'll never take promotion, so I'll have to take your word for it. Anyway, I see you've copped another murder and anything we can do, just ask,' he said with a look of genuine sincerity.

'As it happens, we need you now. Our lead opportunity has done a runner. No idea why he ran, and that's why we played it low key as the bloke who lives there may have nothing to do with either murder, but may have attended the block where Melissa Phelps lived prior to her being killed. Our Intel desk came up with this guy, Buchanan. Anything you can get on him would be good. Especially if he works as a handyman, rides a motorbike and dresses like a dispatch rider. Here's a photo off the net. It's from a webpage he's setup.'

Nash removed the image from her coat pocket and slid the print of Buchanan across the desk. The Silverfox scooped it up and added it to a folder of images.

'Why don't you just call him and get him to come and give you a quote for some work?' he asked, taking a sip of coffee then sniffing the mug before he took another.

'Too soon for that now. He's been spooked, but certainly a consideration should you fail to find him…' Nash said.

'Oh, we'll locate him, but can your lot catch him…? That's the question,' he replied with raised eyes over the rim of his mug.

'Call me as soon as you get anything,' Nash said, as she got up and exited the room.

She returned to her office, hoping she might find some good news there as DCI Carlson wanted an update on each investigation and Nash knew she had little to give that he wouldn't already know by now.

CHAPTER TWELVE

'I know why we're sat here and not Tweedle-Dee and Tweedle-Dumber but, man, it's a drag,' Moretti said to Nash.

They were crouched on the flat roof of the block adjacent to Buchanan's. The evening had turned from dusk to a blanket of darkness. Matthews had established the observation point on the roof and had tasked Begum and Parker with the first shift. Nash had surprised them all by offering to take over after she'd had a call from the source unit. Nash peered at Buchanan's kitchen window. There was no movement.

'Sometimes you have to be the ones with the eyes on if you want the arrest phase to go without a hitch,' she replied, as Moretti tutted and viewed the street using binoculars.

He was pissed off as he'd had plans for the evening, and she'd rained on his parade. Such was life.

'Just keep your eye on the prize and say if you see him. Anyway, you're on overtime whereas muggins here isn't.' Nash fastened down the poppers on her coat and rubbed her gloved hands together.

Despite the weak illumination from the street lamps below, the night sky gave a hint of starlight even though it was early evening. Nash was hoping the Silverfox would call again. This would hopefully happen soon and Nash could move the investigation on as the day had produced little in the way of progress.

She'd had an earlier meeting with DCI Carlson who'd, to use the analogy of a shotgun, used both barrels and may as well have worn a helmet with "Lock 'n' Load" scrawled across it. Nash had pointed out that the lack of progress was due to the early days in what were two murder investigations with little to go on. But he was having none of it. 'Get detecting then,' were his only words of encouragement. He'd had the press bureau on the phone demanding a statement they could release. He'd managed to placate that department, but it wouldn't last for long. They too were getting pressure from the media for information. More so now another murder had happened in the capital.

The streets below changed as night took hold. Dealers emerged and took up their corners; buyers surfaced, bought, and then scurried away like feral rats. Neither

Nash nor Moretti paid any interest in the illegality of the activity and they concentrated on the streets below for signs of Buchanan. After a short while, Nash's phone vibrated in her pocket with a message from the Silverfox – "On way" was all it said.

Nash looked at Moretti. 'We're on – eyes up.'

Twenty minutes later Nash noticed a shadow down by the block. A stooped hooded figure whose face was obscured by a bandana, hugged the wall with their back. The street lamps provided enough light for the binoculars to be of use. Nash gently rotated the focus ring and tried as best she could to steady the view on the new target.

She gestured as to where Moretti should look. He was already focussed and Nash knew he'd clocked the subject as he nodded in recognition. The figure hugged the wall using it as a shield as they moved around to the front entrance. Whoever it was, they were either waiting for an opportunity to buy, or deal, or for the door to the block to open so they could rush in without wasting time opening it. A good criminal knew that time spent outside a locked door could result in them being jumped on from outside. Far better to wait for others to be around, to provide cover and people to push in the way of harm from police attempting to arrest or a rival attempting to assault them.

The motion-activated lights flickered on and illuminated the stairwell of the block. A woman with a buggy bumped the carriage down each step. The subject had seen a strip of grass in front of the block light up and they appeared to ready themself for movement. Nash hoped it was Buchanan and not a mugger. She watched the door to the block open. The woman used the buggy as a prop.

The figure reacted quickly and as the buggy was placed against the door to hold it open, the figure grabbed the opportunity and slipped inside. He took the stairs three steps at a time. This had to be him. Nash watched and waited. The figure emerged on the third floor. They remained at the door to the landing and produced a phone. Nash observed a rapid movement of thumbs then one final press. She couldn't make out the detail on the screen in what she suspected was a message being sent.

This was confirmed as the door to 5C opened. A skinny female dressed in tracksuit bottoms and a thin white T-shirt leaned against the doorframe and lit up. Her frame was illuminated by a light in the flat's hallway. Nash knew a decoy when she saw one. A test to see if police would rush the door. As swift as a hawk drops on prey, the figure emerged from the shadows of the stairwell. The hood was up and bandana still in place. The figure rushed past the female who took one last glance left and right before she threw the cigarette over the balcony and shut the door. The lights in the flat went out and it was cloaked in darkness again.

Nash took out her work phone and dialled a number. The wind was light. She heard the faint whistle across the speaker but not enough to deaden the sound. It was answered quickly.

'Are we on?'

'You're on. Be advised there's another occupant in the flat. Adult female. No other occupants seen. A person entered dressed all in black and very furtive. I'm certain it's our man. You're good to go,' Nash said.

'All received. Enjoy the show,' the voice replied.

Nash looked at Moretti who'd been observing the flat.

'Watch the door,' was all she said, as Moretti scanned the balcony.

At the end farthest from the door he noticed a hatch being lowered from the roof. An emergency ladder that unfurled followed this to the floor. No sooner had it touched the ground than a set of black boots with dark clothing tucked into the top appeared from the hatch space. A figure cloaked in black flameproof overalls slid down the ladder and, once down, secured it with their feet.

More of the same in identical dress descended from the roof and ducked below the lip of the balcony.

Various apparatus were handed down from above: a door enforcer and a metal pole that had a hook on one end and a handle at the other. Short shields were passed and gently placed on the concrete. Once the final officer had descended, the line formed up. It was a formidable makeup of a rapid entry team. The line of officers moved towards the door to 5C with the stealth of a pride of lions readying to attack.

On the count of three, the lead officer dipped his legs and swept up with the enforcer and crashed it into the door. At the same moment, the kitchen windows imploded as other officers smashed through with the metal glass clearers.

The window-smashers stepped aside as another officer went through the window frame into the kitchen screaming 'Police' as they did. The main door caved under the pressure of the enforcer. Both Nash and Moretti were now standing on the roof opposite as shouts and screams could be heard drifting over the night air.

Nash heard a voice shout, 'Stop or I'll release the dog' and as she looked down to the grass, she saw the same dark-clothed figure that had entered the block earlier in a sprint across a green area at the rear. The figure was fast but not fast enough to outrun a German shepherd. The dog sprang from the ground and latched its teeth onto the sleeve of the runner as it brought them unceremoniously to earth. The dog ragged on his arm like a tug toy.

Three other officers in addition the dog handler were now upon the floored figure whose arms were up his back and cuffed. The Landshark lay on its belly. His front legs splayed out as he panted and mouthed a tennis ball. His handler ruffled the dog's head in deep admiration of his partner's robust and swift execution of duty. Moretti turned to Nash as they made their way to their roof's exit point.

'You never fail to surprise me, you said to trust you, and I'm glad I did,' he said, tapping her shoulder as they descended out of the roof by a fixed metal ladder and onto the balcony of their block.

They left their building and walked towards a small crowd that had now gathered, all keen to see what was going on.

'Where we detect, these good people collect. Sometimes we're better off getting the job done properly by those who know what to do,' Nash said.

Moretti smiled and nodded as they walked across the green to where the figure lay in a recovery position to prevent positional asphyxia. The muddied, pissed-off look on the face that stared back at them was that of Neil Buchanan.

CHAPTER THIRTEEN

'You've no right to hold me, you know? I've done nothin' wrong.' Buchanan leaned back in his chair. His feet adorned with plimsolls, courtesy of the police, swung back and forth as though he were a child on a swing. The back of the seat bounced off the interview room wall as he rocked on the back legs. His white paper suit rustled with the movement. A suit that was torn during an altercation with the custody staff over a desire to keep his boots. Boots that were now part of Nash's exhibits.

'Move away from the black strip, would you? Otherwise, the same show will occur as you experienced earlier this evening,' Nash said.

He paused, then returned the front feet of the plastic chair to the grey carpet-tiled floor. Nash detached a

Styrofoam cup from a cardboard cup carrier and pushed it towards Buchanan.

'Tea? Milk, two sugars? I heard you ask the gaoler earlier, but I understand it never arrived after your dance off with the custody officers,' Nash said – his new friend and saviour from hours of further thirst.

'Cheers,' he replied.

The recording started and formalities were exchanged.

'So, why'd you run from police today?' Nash asked.

'I never knew they were police. I thought we were getting burgled.'

'So you ran leaving your girlfriend to confront the offender and take the pain? Very gallant of you,' Nash added.

Buchanan ignored her and kept his concentration on Moretti, avoiding Nash's gaze.

'That's not good enough. I would've thought the shouts of "police" were enough to tell you who was entering your girlfriend's place,' Nash said.

'I don't hear that good.'

'You heard the knocks on your door the other day and that seemed to create the same flight response. It could've been the postman?' Nash said.

'You lot always knock the–' Buchanan stopped and looked at the ceiling then at Nash.

'Look, whatever or whoever it is you're running from, it's all come to a head now. Take this opportunity to talk to us. Who knows, I may be able to help you?' Nash said, a smile across her face.

Buchanan observed Nash as he took a gulp of tea. He placed the drink down, keeping his hands cradled around the cup – the skin taut over his newly grazed knuckles – as though he wanted to throttle it.

'I ran because I owe some people money, that's all.'

'Whom do you owe money to?' Nash asked.

'People. People of no concern of yours,' Buchanan said as he looked at the recorder.

A knock on the door suspended the interview. The tape was left to run as DS Matthews entered. He identified himself for the purpose of the recording and handed Nash a printout from the Police National Computer. Nash scanned it, paused halfway, and looked up at Buchanan. Matthews gave Buchanan a wan smile and left. The door drifted to close.

'Are you certain it's all about money?' Nash said as she handed the printout to Moretti.

'Oh,' came Moretti's response, as Buchanan stayed passive.

Sweat had started to appear on Buchanan's forehead despite his light apparel. They were both aware of what the printout contained and had been since his name had entered the enquiry. Sometimes theatre didn't require the same script and cast to be of enjoyment. Audience participation was everything with this play, and Nash and Moretti milked every drop. Tactics they'd agreed prior to the interview.

'You see, Mr Buchanan, according to the printout we have here, a printout taken from the Police National Computer, you're wanted. Wanted for charging in relation to an attempted murder and rape. This leads me nicely to ask you to account for your movements over the last week: places you've visited, people you've seen… I think you know the score…' Nash said.

Buchanan remained silent. He downed the remainder of his tea and tilted his head to the side.

'I want a brief,' he said.

'Really? We were doing so well,' Nash said.

'I'm not as stupid as you make me out to be. I know what you lot are like. You'll try and get me to talk then fit me up just like the last time.' Buchanan's breathing was becoming laboured as he chewed on his bottom lip.

'Are you happy to carry on or do you actually want a solicitor? Either way works for us,' Nash explained, looking at Moretti then back at Buchanan.

Nash slid the CCTV image over to Buchanan while he considered his options. He glanced down at it then looked up at the ceiling as he pushed it away. The veins in his neck began to pulse.

'Get me a brief and be quick about it,' Buchanan said.

Nash scooped up the CCTV image and turned off the recorder. Moretti waited until they were away from the cellblock before he confronted Nash. They were outside the station canteen when he decided to speak.

'Hang on a minute,' he said as they stopped in the corridor to let others pass them. They stood on opposite sides of the hallway. Moretti stepped forward. 'What went on in there, Pip? Why did you show him the CCTV image?' he hissed.

They'd had a pre-interview meeting and planned how it would go and this hadn't been part of it. Nash waited for a couple of PCSOs to walk past them. Once the swing doors to the canteen came to a rest, she replied.

'Because I needed to see if we were heading in the right direction with the right man, that's why. I've got the Command breathing down my neck for results, quoting stats at me as though I have a degree in maths and want to try for a PhD. The DCI's claiming not enough is being done in relation to our investigation and is asking why we haven't made an arrest or traced any witnesses, that's why. Let's look at the facts, shall we? Buchanan reacted strongly to the image. He knows it's him. By the time his boot print has been matched with that from Melissa Phelps's bathroom floor, we'll be in a much stronger position to nail him than we would've been if the CCTV proved nothing,' she replied. She was firm, but had managed to keep her voice down, conscious of others in the canteen that'd be watching through the squares of glass in the doors.

'Why didn't you suggest that tactic in the pre-interview meet we had?' Moretti pressed.

'Because sometimes, Nick, you just have to act on instinct and that's what I did. If you're not happy with that, there's little I can do about it. Just call his brief and tell him to get here quick. I'll see you back here after you've done it,' Nash said as she pushed through the doors to the canteen leaving Moretti to find a phone to call the solicitor.

'His solicitor's a she, for your information,' he mumbled as the swing doors closed and he walked away.

Moretti made the call and returned to find Nash deep in thought as she flicked through a phone he hadn't seen her with before. He sat opposite her and she put the phone away in her bag.

'*Ms* Norton, from Norton & Co, is on *her* way to see him. She's already intimated on the phone that her client will not be talking again this evening and she's suggested to the custody officer that Buchanan be afforded a rest period before the next interview,' he informed Nash, as he sniffed his tea. Tea that was now tepid.

'Let him fester. Hopefully we'll have something from the lab to put to him in the morning. His solicitor knows why he's been arrested and she can put up with that amount of disclosure, at this stage. Feel free to head back to the office and see what's happening there. I need to see DS Harris before I return,' she said as she got up and left.

Moretti sat back and shook his head. She could be moody when she wanted. Her timing for when she was never ceased to amaze him.

CHAPTER FOURTEEN

Nash sat in her office making some notes when Moretti appeared at her door. He gave the wood a light tap. After last night's performance, he didn't relish waking the sleeping lioness.

'Permission to enter, ma'am?' He strolled in before he'd given her a chance to refuse.

'Did you get enough sleep last night? Your phone call with DS Harris seemed to bother you... your romance on the rocks?' he quipped as he sat down in an easy chair.

Nash looked up and placed her hands behind her head. She swivelled her seat from side to side with her shoeless feet.

'I'm sorry about the way I reacted last night. It was out of order and uncalled for. I've no excuse other than a self-imposed pressure to find the killer for these murders. That and another piece of work with Harris and MO3 that I could've done without, but agreed to nonetheless,' she replied.

Nash brought out her daybook and turned to a page full of scrawl that only she could decipher. They got up and Moretti held the door open for her as they went through to the briefing room where the team was sitting waiting.

Nash nodded at everyone and kicked things off.

'An update from last night: Buchanan was arrested coming out of the rear window to the flats we were at previously. There were no injuries to any officers involved in the arrest. I'm pleased to say that includes police dog, Thor, who valiantly took Buchanan out of the game as he fled.' Nash looked up from her notes to a table of smiles and murmurs of appreciation.

They'd seen the dog handler's body-worn camera footage that had been downloaded for them. The viewing of which had been a team event and could only be described as poetry in motion. It was a delight to behold and a morale booster to her weary team of investigators.

'I do have some other good news... despite his reluctance to talk yesterday, Buchanan was shown the CCTV image from Phelps's block of flats, which he blanked. But he displayed classic body language indicative of being caught on camera. He refused to answer further questions at this point and insisted on seeing a brief. There will be a further interview this morning at 10 a.m. DS Moretti and myself will conduct this.' She paused.

There were no objections, not that she expected any.

'We do have some forensic information that has just been sent through...' she said.

The atmosphere in the room became tense as all of the investigative team waited to see how good this news was.

Nash didn't keep them waiting long. 'The lab has matched samples taken from Melissa Phelps's bathroom floor. Microscopic traces of the bath bomb are on the outside leather of Buchanan's boots. He can try and argue it wasn't from inside her flat but the bath bomb was homemade. By whom, we don't know. It may have been Melissa but from recollection there wasn't anything in the flat to indicate this was a passion of hers. If it wasn't her, then the person who made it will need to be traced and eliminated.'

A couple of the team shifted in their seats. A laborious task if ever there was one. Nash let their voices die down then continued.

'Forensic will be put to Buchanan later.'

Moretti nodded. She hadn't intended to ambush him yesterday. It was just how her mind worked.

'Forensics are *not* for the press or for disclosure outside of this incident room until I say otherwise. He was arrested wearing the boots and the silver buckle is seen on the CCTV. It's a good start for the Phelps murder, at least. Buchanan will have to account for the findings on his boots, and we'll be certain to remind him of the inference a jury could deduce from failing to comment.' Nash paused as notes were taken.

Jonesy was the first to speak up.

'He's gonna say nothing. They always do; but we can say he was in the flat, unless he tries to tell us he lent his boots to someone else! Wouldn't put it past him.'

Nash acknowledged the thought process Jonesy had voiced. She valued her detectives speaking their mind and it was something she actively encouraged.

'The lab's working on his clothing now,' Nash continued. 'The boots were priority. I would expect to find traces of the same on his clothing. If we don't, then we have a problem. Melissa died with a struggle as we've seen from the coloured water pattern on the tiles and wall. We have to hope the clothing he was wearing when he was nicked was the same as in the CCTV picture. A search of the flat he decamped from didn't turn up any other clothing of his, so we have to establish where else he lives and sleeps. The flat is in the name of his girlfriend as the named tenant. In interview, Buchanan claimed to owe money and intimated he didn't know it was police knocking at the door.' Nash stopped as laughter arose like a tsunami around the table. She joined them, as the absurdity of the statement was one she and many of them present had encountered before.

She waited for the voices to desist. She tapped her pen on the desk and they calmed down.

'We're some distance away from a charge. What we have is beneficial, don't get me wrong, but I still want you all to remain open-minded as we pursue this lead. Don't shut your minds down until we are certain we have all the evidence required to get him banged up for life and stay there.'

After the meeting was concluded, Moretti and Matthews remained in the room to discuss action allocations along with Sagona the office manager. Matthews updated the incident room board with the website image of Buchanan and inserted a sign above it that said "Suspect". He sat back down and fired up his computer and logged onto CRIMINT where he typed in Buchanan's full name.

'Now where else have you been getting your head down, me old mucker,' he muttered to himself as he leaned towards the screen.

CHAPTER FIFTEEN

'This interview is being recorded and may be used in evidence if this case is brought to trial. I am DI Nash attached to the Homicide and Serious Crime Command and my colleague is?'

'DS Moretti attached to the same command.'

Nash completed the interview preamble and caution, then Buchanan's solicitor spoke up.

'My client has had sufficient time to discuss matters with me. I have seen the CCTV image you gave in disclosure. I have advised him to make no comment,' she said, as she sat back and waited for the interview to begin.

Moretti had been afforded the opportunity to lead this interview. Nash knew it was a skill that required repetition to be effective.

'Very well, but I will remind your client that it's his choice to act on that advice and his alone. This is your opportunity, Mr Buchanan, to answer the questions we put to you. Questions in relation to a murder which, I'm certain, you appreciate is a serious offence,' Moretti said.

'No comment,' Buchanan responded.

'Can you tell me where you were a week ago today between 5 and 7 p.m.?'

'No comment.'

'Have you ever been to Thamesmere Heights or in the vicinity of that building?'

'No comment.'

'Have you ever been to or entered that block?'

'No comment.'

'Have you ever been to the third floor of that building?'

'No comment.'

'Have you ever been to flat 33c within Thamesmere Heights? A flat that's situated on the third floor?'

'No comment.'

'Mr Buchanan, I will continue asking questions despite the advice you've been given. As I pointed out, it's your choice to say nothing. Remember that before you try and hide behind your solicitor or barrister, as it will be at court, and under oath,' Moretti replied.

'Officer,' Buchanan's solicitor interjected.

'I prefer Detective Sergeant.'

'Very well, Detective Sergeant, are you insinuating that you have enough evidence to charge? If so, I suggest you do so and desist in this charade. I have stated my client's position re answering questions and as much as you have the right to ask them – and I'm in no way saying you shouldn't – my client will not be making any comment.'

Buchanan's tongue flicked out the corner of his mouth like a snake scenting air. Moretti sat back firm in the knowledge it would be he who would taste victory on this occasion.

Moretti looked at Nash who gave him a nod. She leaned down and picked up a docket from between her feet. A docket the solicitor hadn't noticed, and whose eyes now zoned in on. She didn't desist in her tracking as she followed the docket's path from floor to table like an osprey scans a lake ready for the kill. Moretti continued.

'Mr Buchanan, when you arrived at this station you had certain items of clothing removed from you.'

Buchanan looked at his solicitor whose face relaxed with the change of direction. Her eyes widened and her brows rose by way of a reminder for him to remain silent.

'Among those items were a pair of boots. Boots, that have a distinctive silver buckle. Boots that we believe are the same as those seen in the image captured on CCTV.' Moretti paused, purposely taking his time looking in the docket. He waited to see if the solicitor would respond and she did. As Moretti and Nash expected her to.

'I've seen the CCTV image – a very poor one, I might add. There was nothing else disclosed that forensically links my client's boots to that grainy still. If that's where you're going with this interview then my advice remains the same,' she addressed Buchanan, as well as the detectives.

Buchanan nodded as he eyeballed Nash then leaned back in his chair.

'Game set and match, officers,' Buchanan said. A comment that was met with a pursed set of lips from his solicitor and a look that said all he needed to know: Shut up.

Moretti ignored the comment, but noticed Buchanan's neck vein had begun to pulse as it had done when they'd flashed the still image of what they both believed was Buchanan, in the previous interview. Moretti took his time as he produced the lab report from the folder.

'Mr Buchanan, I have a forensic report concerning the examination of your boots. The same boots that were removed from you upon arrest. The same boots this report tells me were also at the murder scene of Melissa Phelps. Boots that have traces of a bath bomb present in the victim's bathroom. The trace could only have come from inside the flat.'

Moretti waited as the front legs of Buchanan's chair hit the floor with fierce determination, his mouth agape as he looked at his solicitor then back at Moretti and Nash. His pupils pulsated as though on a timer as his brain assimilated the information he'd been presented with.

'Would you like a further consultation with your solicitor?' Nash enquired, with an internal glow of satisfaction she hoped was visible to the two sitting across the desk in front of her.

Buchanan looked at his solicitor who nodded that they should talk. Moretti stated the time and suspended the recording leaving the solicitor and Buchanan in the room to digest the latest disclosure.

As Moretti and Nash exited the interview room, Nash turned to him with a smile. 'Tick… tick… boom,' she whispered as she uncurled her fist and splayed her fingers as though showing she carried nothing.

'New balls please,' Moretti replied as they walked with an air of confidence towards the custody officers' podium.

They waited in a vacant consultation room and helped themselves to a pre-packed coffee. Moretti prepped a tea for Buchanan to have on their return.

'Do you think he'll talk?' Moretti asked.

'No. I think he'll stick with his solicitor's advice. That advice will remain the same. Say nothing; see if we disclose anything else,' Nash said. She put down the brown plastic ridged cup and worked her tongue around her mouth and teeth as though she'd ingested noxious fluid.

'How you can drink this stuff, I do not know,' she said to Moretti.

'I got used to it in custody,' Moretti replied.

'Custody?' Nash said.

'Yes, custody. I had a year out on promotion, as there weren't any vacancies in the department for a DS. It was either that or carry on as a DC in a squad that was up for being disbanded. I had a blast. Loved the role but it was hard work,' he said as he topped up his plastic cup with more hot water.

'I would have never had you down as a custody officer. I bet you were a right one to deal with,' Nash replied.

'Thanks for the vote of confidence. I was easy to deal with and the DCs loved me. I knew my stuff. You should've given it a try,' he said, knowing full well Nash had never considered that.

'I was always happiest this side of the desk and getting to see daylight every now and then.'

Moretti smiled. 'I had to take vitamin D supplements in the end as I wasn't getting enough sunlight. I'm certain the community at the marina thought I was a vampire.'

'Very funny. How's things with you and the dancer?' she asked.

'Tabatha? Nothing to report. Haven't seen much of her since Christmas.'

'Oh? From what I've heard you've seen all of her…'

'Well, your source is shit, ma'am. I suggest you ditch them.'

Nash watched him over her cup, but he remained tight-lipped on the subject.

'Do you think you'll see her again?' she asked.

'Who knows? We're both free spirits and this line of work isn't conducive to a relationship, if you ask me,' he said as he finished his drink.

'Neither's getting your tits out while wrapped around a pole, I'd imagine,' Nash said, before the gaoler gave a light knock on the door and informed them the solicitor was ready to resume.

Moretti felt the bell had saved him. He realised he'd felt more comfortable in the interview room than being probed by Nash about his sex life over a crap coffee.

They entered the interview room and resumed in their respective seats. The air in the room resonated hostility as the self-close mechanism on the door engaged and sealed them in. The solicitor had clearly had her work cut out in the time she'd spent with Buchanan since the disclosure. Nash conducted the preamble and it was now her turn to interview.

'So, you've had sufficient time to consider what was disclosed, Mr Buchanan, is there anything you'd like to say by way of explanation? I must remind you that failure to do so in respect of the marks found at the scene may lead to the jury drawing an inference from this, do you understand?'

'Yeah, my brief explained. I've done this statement and that's it. I'm answering nothing else,' Buchanan said. He looked at his solicitor and back at Nash.

'Would you read the statement for me please?' Nash asked.

Buchanan's solicitor picked up the sheet of A4 paper. Nash noted the writing stopped halfway down the page. Not a good sign.

'I've been asked to read this on behalf of my client. These are his words. On February 24th at about six in the evening I went to Thamesmere Heights. I needed to go and collect money owed for some tiling work I'd done on a bathroom there – flat 33. I travel by motorbike and dress appropriately for this purpose. I was carrying a brown bag with sealant just in case any tiling needed touching up. I knocked on the door and it opened. I entered and could see the body of the lady I'd met who owned the flat and owed me the money.

'She was in a bath that was overflowing with water. I could see a lot of water on the floor that was pink in colour. I've watched a lot of crime stuff on TV so I didn't touch anything, but I did step closer to her, as I couldn't believe what I was seeing. The water on the floor was everywhere and splashed as I stepped. I panicked. I tried to wipe it off on a floor mat inside the flat and left closing the door behind me. That's it. I never called the police, as I knew I was wanted. I knew if I did, I'd be nicked for something I never did. I never saw anyone else while I was there.' She finished reading and looked at Nash and Moretti as she placed the statement down.

'So, the door wasn't locked when you arrived?' Nash asked.

Buchanan looked at his solicitor.

'My client has answered that question in his statement, Detective Inspector.'

'With the greatest respect, I am trying to investigate a murder and quite frankly a prepared statement as brief as this doesn't help. Was the door open or closed when you arrived at the flat, Mr Buchanan? I would like you to answer, not your solicitor who wasn't there,' Nash said, as she shot the solicitor a stare.

'Open, but pulled shut like it was closed,' came Buchanan's reply.

'Detective Inspector, your tone is putting adverse pressure on my client to talk. I request this interview be terminated as we have assisted by way of the statement,' his solicitor said.

Nash pressed on.

'What else was in the bag?' Nash asked.

'No comment.'

'Do you have an app on a phone or other device capable of accessing the building and the flat?'

'No comment.'

'How did Melissa Phelps, the occupier of flat 33, contact you in order for the work to be done?'

'No comment.'

'When did she contact you and how?'

'No comment.'

'Did you canvass for work in that area and beyond?'

'No comment.'

Nash took a breath for a beat before she continued, 'I can understand how it may appear to you. Let me reassure you, we work on evidence, Mr Buchanan. If the evidence fits, we will use it. If it doesn't, we will pursue the investigation until we establish it. You are leaving me with little to go on when you admit you were at the scene and we have trace evidence to corroborate that.' Nash paused. She continued to look directly at Buchanan who just shrugged his shoulders and remained mute. 'Very well. I have nothing further to add at this stage. You'll be returned to your cell,' she said.

'How long will I be here for?' Buchanan piped up.

Nash gathered up the papers from the desk and replaced them in a folder before returning her attention to him.

'For as long as the law has given provision, Mr Buchanan. And I will be applying every measure at my disposal to ensure you're not released,' Nash replied, as she terminated the interview.

CHAPTER SIXTEEN

Nash selected a table that provided a clear and unobstructed view of the cafe's door. DS Harris had contacted her an hour before and called the meeting on. It couldn't wait – apparently. Not even a double murder enquiry would frustrate the working machinations of the undercover unit. She checked her watch and as expected Harris was on time. The brass bell hooked over the door announced his arrival. His burly frame cast a shadow over the floor as he stood and scanned the room in search of her. He gave a nod at Nash and weaved through the close-knit chairs to greet her.

'Cheers for coming out. I really do appreciate it,' Harris said, sitting down opposite her and looking over to the counter that housed cakes and sandwiches.

He caught the waiter's eye and ordered two lattes as he could see Nash's was at the dregs stage. Harris took his time to settle in and observed the seating area as he did so. His eyes conducted a final threat assessment of the few who'd decided on the same cafe for a break. Nash was glad she didn't have to live like that on a daily basis anymore. The undercover role was often glamourised in books and films, but the feeling of fight or flight that was a regular torment of the UC's mind was often overlooked.

'I need this hit of caffeine; the traffic was a fucking nightmare,' Harris said as he accepted the cup from the waiter and ignored the tiny handle that would never fit his sausage fingers as he cupped the mug.

'I thought your gym was close to here?' Nash asked.

'It is, I'm going there after this. Chest today and then I'm having a rest day. The old body's not taking the damage like it used to when I was younger.' Harris took a sip of coffee and wiped the milk from his upper lip as he leaned towards Nash.

'Our piece of work's going well. Foot traffic's good and the deliveries are spot on and regular, just like we wanted. He's a good contact, your man,' Harris said.

Nash deciphered the words to mean the gang of phone robbers had been active and sending business into the sting shop.

'Good to hear. So, what now?' she enquired, with a degree of hesitation in her voice. She had hoped her role with Harris was over.

'Well… thing is… our associate has been asking after you. Let's say he liked your introduction and wondered if you had any others, like me, he could link up with to open his distribution network to an even wider audience,' Harris said, eyeing a protein bar that appeared out of place amongst the cakes.

'Tell him you haven't seen me in a while. You'll pass the message on should I get in touch,' Nash said.

Harris laughed but not loud enough to encourage unwanted attention from the other occupants of the cafe, all of whom were engrossed in their own worlds. Worlds dictated by their phones. The barista wiped down the coffee machine and selected a mug to dry from a dishwasher.

'I thought you'd be up for a bit more fun? Like the old days. Well, not like those days but you get my drift. All this death and murder is getting you down, Pip, look at ya?'

Nash side-eyed Harris whose attention was now drawn to the window and a traffic altercation that was occurring outside.

'Where's uniform when you need them, eh? Stuck indoors dealing with shite when they should be out on foot dealing with dickheads like these two,' Harris said, as he returned his attention to Nash.

Nash answered his pearls of wisdom.

'You need a spell out of your world too. You have no idea the pressures everyone's under. According to your vision of the Met everyone's there to serve you when actually you're here to serve us,' Nash said.

Harris coughed into his hand and muttered an obscenity at the same time.

'How are the jobs going anyway? Rumour control says you've nicked someone already who's as good as convicted?' he said.

'I can put him at the scene but can't say he committed murder.'

'I've charged on less than that, what's your problem?' Harris said.

Nash shook her head at Harris's attitude.

'It's remarks like that, Carl, that will ensure you remain where you are,' she said.

Harris smiled and chuckled to himself. He nodded at the barista and pointed at the protein bar in an expression of appropriation.

'Look, we've all got our strengths and mine happens to be with the criminal elements of society. I get on fine in that world without crossing the line. I know where I stand, which is more than can be said for our organisation,' Harris said as he accepted the protein bar from the barista.

'Anyway, the other reason I called was to give you a couple of phones now that I've got the bent ones you bought.' Harris grinned and he delved into the inner pocket of his denim jacket. He produced an old Nokia and passed it to Nash who picked it up and examined it.

'It doesn't work!' she exclaimed as she tried turning it on.

The screen remained blank. Harris sat back like his work was done and he'd earned a holiday.

'It works a treat, let me tell you,' Harris said as he leaned closer to her and took the phone in his palm.

'Consider this a gift from me to you for all your dedication to the cause.'

'Carl, it doesn't work, that's obvious. Where's the charger, you cheapskate? It may be out of battery,' Nash asked.

'It works fine. It gives the appearance to the untrained eye that it's defective.'

Harris glanced about then spoke. 'Look, carry this with you and if you're ever in bother all you need to do is bring up in conversation where you are and what the score is and the cavalry will come running,' Harris said, like it was all so simple.

Nash decided to play the game and gave him a look that expressed genuine interest but was far from it.

'So, it's voice activated and linked to the main control room?' she asked with a hint of sarcasm.

'Don't be silly. I don't like you that much. Look, I know that one of the reasons you're reluctant to work with me is that the backup just isn't there anymore. I get it. The operational teams do their best but more often than not we go in alone. With this gadget you at least have the chance of getting some help should you need it,' Harris said, with a note of assurance in his voice.

'So, if it isn't linked to any police control room, how will it help me?' she questioned.

'Simple. If we go out on a job and I get called away–'

'As you usually do,' she interjected.

'Yeah, yeah. Well, all I have to do is call this phone and the line goes live. I can hear everything being said and if needs be co-ordinate the cavalry or make an assessment, you'll be fine. Either way, if chummy picks it up it looks like a dead phone, like you assumed, so what do you reckon? Will you accept the gift and think about taking it out when we're together?'

Harris slid the phone back across the table to Nash who placed it in her coat pocket along with two other phones that operated normally. Anyone watching would have thought it a strange transaction but it wouldn't do their reputation any harm if a criminal had observed them.

'I've taped the number on the back of the cavalry phone. Remove it before you carry it. Give the number to any other female on your team, as I know I'd be punching above my weight with you,' Harris said with a smirk.

'I'm sure your wife would be overjoyed with me facilitating that,' Nash replied.

Harris rolled his eyes and stuck his tongue in his cheek as he checked his watch.

'I've gotta shoot but please consider meeting our man in the phone shop again. This job's working out to be bigger than anyone expected and it would help me out too,' Harris said before he downed his coffee and got up to leave.

'I've got these,' he said as he saw Nash produce a twenty-pound note from her purse.

Nash nodded her thanks knowing full well Harris would claim it all back on expenses.

She watched him leave. Not out of affection, but to ensure he wasn't being followed. She continued as far as her eyes would allow through the main window from where they'd been sitting. She felt the phones in her coat and rolled one around her fingers. She picked up her work phone and called DS Matthews.

'Anything back from billing on the victims' phones?' she asked.

'I'll check, just wait a mo.'

Nash waited while her ear filled with the rustle of paper and the bang of desk drawers. Finally, Matthews came back on.

'Yes, we do. Shall I leave it on your desk?'

'Give it to Moretti. I'll see him later and go through it with him, cheers,' she said.

She hung up and gathered herself together to leave. Before doing so she messaged Moretti: 'Free to meet in next hour?"

She waited, then a reply came through.

Yes. I'm with Owen and have the papers. See you at usual place?

"Great," she replied as she left one cafe and headed for another.

CHAPTER SEVENTEEN

The sun graced Nash's face as she strolled towards the Tate Modern.

She'd made use of the Tate Modern as a DC when out getting statements or on lab runs when Lambeth was the Met's home for forensics. As a UC, she'd always come here before a meet if she was leaving straight from the police station in order to relax and desensitise from policing before she had to change role to whatever act was required. Today was different. Her timing was impeccable as Moretti was parking the car he'd arrived in, and placing a police vehicle logbook in the window. Nash joined him and they entered the building together.

They found a quiet table in the restaurant area, ordered a bottle of water and sat back.

'So, have you had any chance to look at the phone data? I appreciate that may be a tall ask,' she said as she poured Moretti some water from the recyclable glass bottle before supplying her own glass.

'I haven't, but I did catch five minutes with Owen. He said he'd scanned through them and there was nothing obvious screaming from the pages. He's still got his team looking at where Melissa's personal phone was purchased. Her work mobile was ordered through her company from a high street phone provider,' Moretti said.

He took a sip of water and wished it was a Stella Artois. He passed Nash a photocopy of the data.

'This is phone data from Melissa's personal phone,' he said.

Nash took it and started reading down the list of numbers.

'You're right, there isn't much here at all. I recognise the contact details for her parents and – here – the number that was being used by Buchanan. It was on the business card he used.' She pointed to the number and showed Moretti on his copy.

'So he'd contacted her two days before she died, at 6:15 p.m. The call was brief so it could've been to arrange a meeting or confirming one?' Nash questioned.

She looked up at Moretti who was engrossed in his own sheet. She was thinking why DS Matthews hadn't picked up on it, but she put it down to human error due to the long hours they'd endured.

'Could be. If it was Buchanan who killed her, he's not interested in calling to confirm she's in as he'd only have had a mobile number and she could've been anywhere,' Nash said, rattling a Bic biro between her teeth. She stopped as she could see Moretti was getting annoyed at the sound and continued.

'We do know the location where the call was made from though. This is the cell site data from Buchanan's phone that was found on him when he was nicked,' Moretti said as he handed her another sheet of paper.

Nash glanced down the sheet and looked up at him.

'If I'm reading this right then the phone triangulation puts the call coming from a mast closest to Buchanan's girlfriend's address. How far is that from Melissa's flat?' Nash asked.

Moretti brought up Google Maps and checked the address and the route by car.

'By motorbike he could easily be there within ten minutes,' he said.

Nash considered the information before commenting. Whether this was relevant or not was too early to say and Buchanan wasn't going to be explaining much more to them anyway.

'So he wasn't that far from the victim's block, and we know where his phone was when the call to the victim was made two days prior to her death. Let's get JJ over to the girlfriend's flat and see what she has to say. Get him to put some pressure on to establish Buchanan's movements. I'm aware she was spoken to on the night of his arrest but this is new information. She may choose to help now the dust has settled and he's out of her flat. She didn't seem too upset at his arrest from what I heard,' Nash said.

Moretti made a note in his daybook as Nash continued.

'Jonesy tried to have a month's worth of CCTV footage recovered from the block's hard drive to see if he could ascertain if Buchanan had been working there as he'd said. Unfortunately, the hard drive was too corrupted the further back it went. It's un-viewable in terms of quality. He's searched through what he can but he's not hopeful. The concierge is non-committal as to whether he'd seen Buchanan on any occasion in the block. Jonesy showed him the image from the website and the concierge wasn't forthcoming. I don't understand how a block with residents who clearly have money wouldn't be concerned that the CCTV for the building was crap and the concierge was as useful as a cardboard cut-out!'

Moretti nodded in agreement.

'So where do we go from here, DI Nash?'

'Is it down to the lake I fear…?'

'Very good. I never had you down as a Haircut One Hundred fan?'

'There's so much you don't know about me, DS Moretti… so much you don't know,' Nash joked. 'Any news from Buchanan's solicitor?'

'Only asking when we plan to let him out and when he can get his property back. She either believes he's innocent or she's incredibly naive. My money is on the former. Our evidence is weak, Pip. We only have the evidence on Buchanan's boot and some phone data that only amounts to where his phone was at the time a call was made to Melissa Phelps. We can't say for certain it was Buchanan that made the call despite having no reason to believe it wasn't him. He clearly prized his phone, as he was reluctant to give it up on arrest. Owen plans to get a DC on his team to work on the numbers shown in the log and ascertain whom they belong to. He felt, from your call, you wanted to see the data sooner rather than later.'

Nash shrugged by way of reply. Moretti broke her thoughts.

'Buchanan's provided an explanation as to why he was at the flat. There's evidence that recent tiling work has been done in the bathroom. Work he intimated he'd done and was seeking payment for. He's either being very clever and targeted two women who needed bathroom work doing or he's telling the truth,' he said to Nash, who leaned back and rubbed her temples as she considered Moretti's reasoning.

'Possibly. At present he's all we've got. He could be telling us the truth, or his solicitor has prepped him on the statement and answers he should give with the knowledge of what a forensic scientist would look for in the circumstances. She could've provided him with ideas as to why he'd have been in her bathroom and how he was likely to react once he'd realised this was the case,' Nash replied.

Her phone rang. She answered and the dulcet tones of the Silverfox rang in her ears.

'Pip, I have something for you,' he said.

Nash covered the mouthpiece with a cupped hand.

'Is it our murder weapon with a suspect and a taped confession that will stand up in court?' she said.

The Silverfox chuckled. 'I thought you already had that?'

Nash heard him laughing down the phone before he recovered and continued.

'Sadly not, but we've had information about a lockup used by your man Buchanan. I'll message the address and pass everything else to Owen, DS Matthews, I mean.'

Nash motioned for Moretti to pass her some paper.

'Go on,' she said, and wrote down the address on a napkin as Moretti refused to tear a page out of his book.

'What am I likely to find there?' Nash enquired, with a note of caution to her voice.

'Nothing that would cause you extra work, so I'm told, but obviously my individual hasn't been in there, they've just heard he has access to it.'

'Access?'

'Yes.'

'Well, does he own it, rent it, or is he squatting?' Nash probed.

'Let's just say my friendly is satisfied that he is the sole user,' the Silverfox stated.

'Thank you. I will get on it,' Nash said and terminated the call.

Moretti put his empty glass down on the table.

'Our invaluable source unit?' Moretti said.

'The very same. We have a lockup Buchanan uses. Cancel that JJ visit to the girlfriend for now. We'll wait until the lockup has been searched and reassess,' Nash said.

Moretti hadn't made contact with JJ so all was good. They finished up and after a coffee they left and returned to the car.

CHAPTER EIGHTEEN

The lockup was a single garage in a long block. Its up and over door was newly fitted and looked to be part of a planned refit by the council. Buchanan's girlfriend, Tiffany, stood with Moretti, Nash and JJ. She'd sniffed on being passed the search warrant and handed over a set of new keys on a wire ring to JJ. She followed them down to the block where she pointed out her garage door that JJ opened.

'You've obviously got fuck all better to do than harass my partner and me while a lunatic is out killing women,' Tiffany drawled in her North London twang.

Nash ignored her and concentrated on JJ.

Tiffany refused to enter the garage and insisted she remained outside to smoke. Nash nodded at Moretti who got the picture he should join her, while Nash, JJ, and DC Mellor from the outside enquiry team conducted a search of the garage.

At the back of the garage was an old freshly painted Honda 250cc, with a metal rear rack and panniers attached to the sides by bungee cords. Perched on top of the rack was a crash helmet. The helmet was similar in appearance to the one on the CCTV.

Once they'd set the search parameters in their heads, they doubled up their barrier gloves, put on forensic oversuits, and began the task required. JJ started with the outside frame of the garage door as he began the search. It was imperative they were thorough. After a short duration he arrived at the Honda. It was balanced on its central stand. He dipped into a crouch as he visually examined the bike. The fuel cap was a temporary replacement that just pulled out, and as he released it, he could see the petrol sloshed in the tank via his torch and the smell confirmed it was fuel. He plugged the tank and continued to search the rest of the frame and engine until he finally came to the seat and panniers.

The panniers were a plastic set that draped over the metal-tubed frame of the rack. They were secured to the rack by a new bungee cord. JJ raised the pannier lid and directed the torchlight inside and moved the beam in a figure of eight.

'Whoa,' he announced.

Everyone stopped. They looked over to where JJ stood. Mellor peered over JJ's hunched shoulders. He stuck his head over the pannier behind the torch JJ held. Mellor looked back at Nash who was at the entrance to the garage.

'What is it?' Nash enquired.

JJ took out his mobile phone and snapped an image using the phone's flash and the torch Mellor now held for him to illuminate the pannier's dark interior. He looked at the capture while he walked over to where Nash was standing. Moretti kept Tiffany distracted as best he could, but JJ's reaction hadn't been lost on her.

Nash stared at the screen then expanded it with her thumb and index finger. The pixels knitted together to show a roll of duct tape, a short length of rope, a balaclava, leather gloves and a Stanley knife with the blade exposed.

Nash leaned into JJ's neck.

'Get Yvonne down here,' she said. 'I want the bike lifted and brought in. I've not known many handymen who travel with that kind of kit in their panniers. I've seen this kind of get-up on a previous rape investigation where the offender had a happy bag – his words, not mine. I'd put money on that lot being a kit to facilitate rape. We need to know if it's been used and on whom.'

She looked back at where Tiffany was standing and approached her. Moretti waited.

'Do you use that garage?' Nash asked.

Tiffany stood with a cigarette held high between her index and middle fingers. Her nails were speckled with chipped pink nail varnish. Smoke drifted by her right ear and weaved through her matted blonde hair as the breeze caught the vapours of death. She made a pathetic attempt to look beyond Moretti to where JJ now stood. Tiffany's head rolled on her neck as though she was acting the part of a drugged swan in a badly funded play.

'What would I use the place for? I ain't got a motor… he used it for his work stuff and to store his bike. There are thieves about or didn't ya know?'

'Who do you mean by *he*?' Nash asked.

'My fella, the one you lot nicked and the reason why you're here.'

'Anyone else have access to it?' Nash asked.

'Not that I know of. What he does with it is his business and nothing to do with me,' Tiffany replied, taking a long drag on her cigarette. She inhaled the smoke deep into her lungs before expelling it over her shoulder through chapped, rouged lips.

Nash looked back at the garage then back to Tiffany.

'Do you know why he ran from police?' Nash asked.

'Yeah, he's wanted. You lot must know about that by now,' Tiffany replied.

'What did he tell you he was wanted for?' Nash probed.

'He said he'd been nicked for theft and not gone back on bail,' Tiffany explained with an apathetic drone that was supposed to convey an air of confidence as she nibbled on her bottom lip.

There was hesitancy in her voice. Hesitancy Nash had heard many times before.

'He lied to you, Tiffany. He's wanted for rape. Rape of a seventeen-year-old girl. A rape at knifepoint,' Nash said, and paused to let the message sink in.

Tiffany's eyes darted from Nash to Moretti as she sought clarification of what she'd just heard. Neither detective spoke the words of reassurance she desired. Her volatile reaction said it all.

'You're fucking lying. He'd never do anything like that. He ain't like that. He just goes out to work then comes home,' she said.

She blinked rapidly in an attempt to dispel her tears. Tears that now flowed down her pockmarked cheeks. She sniffed and rubbed her face with her arm. Nash motioned to JJ to hand her his phone, which he did. Nash found the photo of the pannier's contents and turned the screen towards Tiffany.

'I'm not in the habit of lying to people, Tiffany,' Nash said. 'This is what's in the pannier. There's nothing there that reassures me he's being truthful. Does that look like what you'd expect him to use at work?'

Tiffany looked at the image, her eyes in a thousand-yard stare. Nash waited. The pain of broken trust needed to reveal itself mercilessly.

Tiffany attempted to avert her eyes, but she couldn't. All she could do was stare. Her legs wobbled and her body shivered. Nash sensed she was about to drop and took hold of her arms. Her tears fell along with inconsolable sobs of grief. Grief at the deception she'd lived under, and the myth of the decent human being she thought Buchanan was. All her dreams of a settled life with the man she'd trusted and loved shattered. Tiffany sniffed, then spat the contents that had entered her throat into the concrete rain gulley.

'It probably ain't his,' she said. 'He must've been looking after it for a mate. Means nothing. I've got shit to be getting on with so drop the keys back once you're done destroying my life.'

Tiffany threw her cigarette butt down and ground it in with a brief twist of her Converse. As she walked away her shoulders juddered with every heavy step she took.

CHAPTER NINETEEN

Moretti collapsed into his favourite leather tub chair and gazed at the tumbler of whiskey. The day had been long but rewarding. They'd re-interviewed Buchanan who'd maintained his solicitor's advice of no comment and stuck to it this time. No explanation for the contents of the pannier, which were now in the system for forensic examination. They hoped something would come back that would lead to a further charge against Buchanan even if it wasn't related to their investigations.

An internal appeal had been raised and placed on the Police Intranet system with the hope that any borough that was dealing with a serious sexual offence that factored rope, tape and a knife, should contact Nash's team. They were running out of time to hold Buchanan. Nash would have to make a decision whether to charge or bail soon, or to consult with the CPS with what they had.

Moretti noticed an internal light was on in Tabatha's boat. He toyed with his glass and grabbed the bottle and another tumbler. He wanted company that wasn't a police officer, but quickly realised it wouldn't be a good idea. He needed a clear head for tomorrow and on previous encounters with Tabatha that had proved a rarity. He'd met with Jade Williams's parents' today and it had been a tough meeting. Many questions had been asked as to the strategy the team had, and whether they were linking the two cases together as they'd read of a similar murder in the *Metro* paper. He'd managed to assuage them as best he could. Nash was unavailable but knew he wouldn't be able to maintain that position for long. They needed results and fast. Moretti had stood the team down at 8 p.m. He was aware that some of the staff were in need of an evening at home and as both cases were in the same state, he saw no reason why they shouldn't. Nash would've done the same, he was sure, and he'd seen no reason to bother her.

He got up, found his bag and took out his daybook and pen. He took both along with his drink over to a sofa near to his turntable. He placed everything he'd carried on a low table and flicked through his albums until he found one that suited his mood and requirement to think. Otis Redding was his choice of company.

He gently extracted the vinyl from its paper bed and placed the record on the turntable's felt mat. He lowered it carefully, as though he was placing a sleeping baby back in a cot. He let the needle drop and sat back down. He picked up his book and pen and found a page with a comparison diagram he'd drawn up of the two victims' lifestyles. The only similarities being they were professional women, single, lived and worked in London and owned a cat. He put it back down, picked up the phone and called Tabatha.

* * *

Nash had just started to boil some pasta after a Wing Chun workout with the wooden dummy training tool that occupied a corner of her living room. Her covert phone's screen blinked for attention. The name Denny appeared on the screen. It was Harris. Nash had his pseudonym programmed into her phone. It helped her remember to use it. Nash glided her thumb across the screen to answer.

'What you up to?' Harris asked in a jovial but inquisitive tone. Nash recognised his voice.

'I'm at home, trying to eat after a workout, you?'

'Well put him down. I'm at the coalface and need some help.'

Nash ignored the remark and kept the phone at her ear as she stirred the pasta.

'You're kidding me? I've been in senior management meetings since I left a search and I'm knackered. Is there no other poor sod you can drag out at this time of night to get you home?' Nash said.

'I wish, but sadly not. Your man has called. He wants another meet but insists on you being there. Look, I know it goes against the grain and you've done what was asked, but it should be a quick ten-minute link then away. He's a little skittish now business is up and running between us. He wants to know you're still in the picture to hold his hand. Not that I'm suggesting you'd wish to. So, how about I get you in… five minutes?'

'Are you outside my flat?' Nash asked.

She looked out of her living room window where she saw the unmistakable form of DS Harris waving back at her, all smiles and confidence.

'Where else would I be? Shift your arse, Pip, and don't wear anything fancy.' Harris laughed.

Nash shook her head in his direction and let the curtain drop. She killed the gas and the boiling water cut to a simmer. She dressed in a loose pair of yoga trousers and a warm top to match. She slipped on some trainers and grabbed a body warmer. She grabbed the phones Harris had given her. She hadn't explained the number to Moretti yet as she'd had other priorities to address, but she hoped she wouldn't be in need of it tonight.

Nash jumped in the back seat of Harris's car and spread out across the length of the seats. Harris was a stickler for cleanliness, as were most of the villains he associated, professionally, with. Cars that appeared clear of crap were less likely to be searched, or so the theory went. As Harris drove, Nash stared out at the lights of London. She wondered whether she'd get a spark of light that would capture the essence of her own investigations and shine the way towards a suspect and a result at court. Not that she could do anything about that at present, but such was the flexibility the job expected of its officers, regardless of rank, when specialist work required immediate attention.

Harris prepared for the meeting by listening to music on the car's stereo and kept himself to himself as he drove. Every now and then he'd glance in the rear-view mirror. Nash knew this was only to make sure she was awake, or to make certain they weren't being followed. They arrived at the shop in good time. Nash sat up and glanced over at the shop window. She felt safe to observe thanks to the privacy glass in the car. A slither of light provided by the cracks in the shuttered frame indicated someone was in. All good, so far, she thought.

Harris dumped the car in a side street and they walked around to an alleyway at the rear of the shop. He casually strode towards a steel reinforced door; an entrance he'd obviously used before as he hit the steel with the side of his fist. Mace answered it quickly and they entered. He embraced Harris like a long-lost friend and Harris reciprocated. Nash declined Mace's advances by folding her arms as though she was cold. They were shown into a small back room.

Mace opened a door onto a set of wooden steps that descended into a basement area. He went first. Nash and Harris followed.

'For my own piece of mind put any phones on the table and remove batteries,' Mace said as he pointed at chairs that surrounded a wooden table for them to sit. Harris emptied his pockets and placed two phones down.

Nash brought out the Nokia Harris had given her and an identical iPhone Harris had acquired to replace hers. Mace's eyes fixed on the Nokia. She ignored him despite seeing his attention drawn to it. She put it down to a habit of his trade. Nash made a show of turning her iPhone off. Mace reached above a run of cabinets and produced a metal detection wand similar to the ones used in the custody area.

'A small precaution before we begin.' He gesticulated with the wand for Harris to raise his arms to the side.

Harris looked away and raised his arms nonchalantly. Nash shook her head and tutted but did the same. Mace, now satisfied, began to relax and moved to place the wand away.

'Not so fast,' Nash said.

Mace paused, mid stretch, and turned back to face her.

'Now it's your turn. I need to be satisfied the way is clear for conversation,' she said. She smiled at the owner and widened her eyes.

Mace shrugged and handed the wand to her. Nash handed it to Harris. There was no way she was getting close to the sweating bulk of Mace. Harris took the wand and handled the scan. Mace lowered his arms and once Harris had finished, he handed the wand back.

'We're good to go,' Harris acknowledged.

Mace poured each of them a drink and raised his glass.

'To business, salute,' he said before downing the drink.

Harris raised his glass and took a sip. Nash left hers alone. Mace looked at her as if he'd been insulted.

'I like to keep a clear head while business is discussed,' Nash assured him.

Mace shrugged but accepted the explanation.

'So, I have good news for you, my friends. I have another supplier who is interested in coming on board with our profit-sharing venture. They have a steady flow of product that will service each of our premises well. In this day and age too many people like to talk to police and it is only a fool who keeps all his stock in one place, no?' Mace said, while raising his palms towards the two of them and cocking his head.

Harris nodded in agreement and waited for him to continue. The more he let him talk the better it was for his investigation. Harris wasn't wired because he had Nash to corroborate anything said, if it came to that. He was very glad he wasn't after Mace's apparent change of tactic. Harris breathed deeply. It was all going better than he expected and he felt relaxed enough in the company to know he wouldn't be needing backup tonight. This was a good thing as there wasn't any. For the moment this was just an exploratory sit-down and nothing more. See what was being offered and take things from there.

'What kind of product are we talking about?' Harris asked, keen to establish they were still singing off the same hymn sheet.

'IPhones, the latest. All boxed and ready to go. We will make sure each one is unlocked to any network. I am assured they are, but you can't trust some people to be telling the truth,' he said, shaking his head.

Harris nodded his appreciation while he stifled a laugh. If only the owner knew. Harris also knew Nash would not stop laughing if he set her off, so he took a deep breath, coughed and bashed his chest.

'Sorry, strong stuff that,' Harris said as he pointed at his glass.

'It is my own vodka brought over by family when they last visited home. So, are you in the market for expansion? Price we negotiate, but what you say?'

Harris looked at Nash who gestured with a flick of her chin that it was down to him to take the decision. Nash had made a point of saying as little as possible. Last thing she wanted was for Mace to believe her presence would be at every meeting. She'd enough of her main work to deal with, and she felt a nagging guilt that she wasn't focussed on it now.

'Show me what you've got,' Harris said.

'I knew you'd want to see for yourself before making decision. You're a wise man,' Mace said as he rose up and went to a cupboard.

He produced a sealed box and brought it to the table.

'This one is for you. A gesture of goodwill and you can see they are legit. All top of the range.' Mace pushed the sealed box towards Harris.

Harris tapped the box with his fingers as he mulled over what was being requested. He bided his time as to whether he would open it or play it a different way. He was conscious of giving the appearance he was who he was purporting to be, a man much like Mace. This was no street drug deal.

'You've been straight with me since our mutual friend here introduced us. I also know where you operate. I've no reason to think these phones are anything but the real deal. One question,' Harris said.

'Go on.'

'How can I be confident they won't come back on me or anyone I sell them to?'

'My boy will make sure they are all set up and the boxes resealed. Professionally, of course, you understand. Like the one you have now. This isn't the first time we have worked this system. It is tried and tested. Nothing to worry about for you or the customer. They get the latest in perfect condition. So, what you say? Name the volume of units you require.'

Harris sat back and turned the box over in his hands as though he was preparing to throw an American football. Harris had him just where he wanted him. He knew this wasn't Mace's first foray and was grateful he'd admitted as much. There'd been a series of lorry thefts where pallet-loads of phones were robbed. An inside man had been put in the warehouse by a crime family. They in turn learned which transport took which products and the route. All that was left was for the driver to be relieved of the cargo before it reached its destination.

What the family hadn't bargained for was a team of undercover officers to work the same warehouse and plant a shipment of phones on a rigged lorry. Rigged for sight and sound. Harris knew where this phone had come from because the last three digits on the serial number of the box told him this was from the last lorry jacking. The driver was an undercover police officer. The cameras mounted all over the lorry cab and container recorded the rest, as did the surveillance team who'd observed the robbery with the knowledge there was to be no arrests at that stage. Now Harris had the last link in the chain, the man who sold them on. All was looking good in DS Carl Harris's world.

'I'll take eighty percent of what you've got, and you hold twenty. That way the risk is on me and not you. But I'll need the profit split in my favour,' Harris said as he waited for the bartering to begin.

Nash, who was as much in the dark as Mace, sat back and observed the play. Business was as good as done and she didn't need any long celebration.

'Sixty-forty in my favour as I have taken the greater risk in obtaining the product. I will have the units delivered to you at the end of the week,' Mace said, reaching across the table to shake hands with Harris who'd nodded in agreement.

Harris beamed inside, as he knew the reason for the delay in delivery. It was down to the warehouse where they were stored being in Kent. He knew this, as that was where the phones had been taken after the robbery, and the place was now under police observation. Harris now knew they'd all be moved sooner rather than later and the operational team would be overjoyed that the job was panning out better than they'd all hoped at the start.

Nash stood up. Harris took the opportunity she'd presented to make their exit and conclude business. Mace went to place his hand on Nash's shoulder but she deftly ducked away.

'I'm all sweaty after a run. A pleasure to do business as always,' she said, as she smiled and went for the door Harris held open.

'I knew you were a shrewd woman the first time I saw you,' came Mace's reply as he watched her leave, closely followed by Harris.

* * *

Their car was still where they'd left it. Home was exactly where Nash was going and not on a celebratory bender with Harris. She got in the passenger seat this time and Harris knew she'd something she needed to voice.

'You knew what that meet was going to be about didn't you?' she enquired, as they stopped at the first set of lights they met.

'What do you mean?'

'Just how far down the road is your operation, Carl?'

Harris wiped his mouth and checked the side mirror before moving off.

'Look, you won't be in any evidential chain. Not with the evidence the Ops team have on this firm. I needed you there tonight and it was a huge success as—'

'As you knew that boxed phone was nicked and which job it was from. You had all the evidence you required sat in your bear-like paws,' Nash said, looking side-on at Harris as he drove.

'What's eating you?' he asked.

'What's eating me is that you dragged me along to a meeting you knew was going to go your way despite the fact I told you I have a double murder investigation on my books. I only came because you said it would ease matey boy's mind if he saw me again. Well, from what I could see, he didn't need any reassurance. You pulled me along on one of your jollies for what? To gloat? Give it the big I am? What the hell's got into you?' Nash said.

Harris checked his rear-view mirror. He'd heard enough. He swung the car over outside a kebab shop. People lingered on the pavement and the staff looked hassled.

'Out with it, Pippa, because I'm not up for a car journey with you chewing at my ear because your investigation has hit the skids where mine happens to be taking off. We're all under pressure for results. Contrary to what you may think, I know you understand the role and know when to shut up. If you can't take the responsibility of the undercover world anymore just say and I'll revoke your ticket. Shame though, as that course isn't cheap,' Harris said.

'Isn't cheap? It's you and Tiny that run it and you make money off it too!'

'Bollocks! That money is for fuck-up fines and it all goes to charity, and you know it. So, what's up?'

Out here they were the same. Rank didn't matter. They were still hyped up from the meeting and not back in the role of being police. Nash ruffled her hair and let the seat's neck rest support her head as she stared ahead.

'I enjoyed tonight, all right. I miss this work. Those carefree times where results mattered but no one was dead at the end of it. No grieving families and answers you can't give. It's the first week of March and my team have had no downtime from the last job. They're on their knees but still doing all they can. I feel knackered, if I'm honest, and could make a mistake if I'm not careful.'

'Like Pussygate you mean?'

Nash looked at Harris who had his eye on a set of legs that extended from a short skirt that had drifted into the kebab house.

'Exactly. JJ is one of the best I have. It's just not like him to make those kinds of errors. Even Moretti had a pop at me the other day and it's been ages since he's done that.'

Harris withdrew his gaze from the legs and back into the car. He'd been listening. He'd never ignore a friend even if his body language indicated otherwise.

'For what it's worth I do remember the days of running a team, not murder, pro-active,' he said. 'It was easier then.

I had the staff and the cash to give out as much overtime as we could muster. Times have changed, Pip. The staff and the money ain't there anymore, as we both know. Especially being a DI. I stay in this role because I love it. I get a buzz from it. When I get jobs like these, I know I'm doing decent work so I don't give a fuck about anything else. Probably why I'm out here now and not at home. You're different though. You've got brains and you're a decent copper who cares. Just don't let the bastards grind you down.' Harris finished speaking and let out a sigh. More from tiredness and a release of adrenaline now the night's work was done.

'Kebab for old times' sake? On me?' Harris asked.

'You never did know how to show a woman a good time did you, Carl? That would be lovely. I'm sure the Commissioner wouldn't begrudge us getting fed.'

CHAPTER TWENTY

The warmth of the sun was weak, but Nash accepted its energy with grace. The magistrate's court had been stuffy and dark as she exited the court building with a warrant for further detention. Buchanan's solicitor had been present. Buchanan was going nowhere but his cell. Nash's team had seventy-two hours to obtain the crucial evidence to make a charge stick tighter than an overwound screw. Her gut reminded her she had some way to go as she ducked into a bakery and grabbed a coffee before she hit the tube for the journey back to base.

Her evening with DS Harris had been a good tonic. She'd been reminded that undercover work could have its moments, but for the majority of the time it could be as frustrating as investigating murder. The residual taste of kebab hung on her tongue like the scent of a sudden death. She hoped the caffeine would cake her tongue and blast the final remnants of taste from the previous evening into history. She felt her suit jacket pocket vibrate.

She took out her phone. The screen said "Sherlock".

'Morning, Nick, I hope you're well?'

A laboured breathing filled her ear as she pressed the phone closer to her skin. She could hear the sound of traffic in the background. He must be on foot, or running for a bus, she thought. She hoped it wasn't an arse dial, as she needed to update him on the events at court. It wasn't.

'Have you left court?' Moretti asked.

'I'm headed back to the office, what's up?'

'Don't. I need you at St Thomas's Hospital. A female presented there last night. She's alleged a male wearing a ski mask raped her three weeks ago. Her hands were bound, mouth gagged, and she was threatened with a Stanley knife. The venue's an alley near a block of flats not a million miles from where Buchanan has been getting his head down.'

Nash had stopped walking to ensure she didn't lose their connection. She looked around for a black cab. The quicker she got to the hospital the better.

'Who's with her now?' she asked.

'A SOIT officer from a borough Sapphire team. The ones specially trained to deal with victims of sexual offences. She'd seen the Intranet appeal and called the incident room once she'd heard the victim's initial account,' Moretti explained.

Nash knew what a SOIT officer was but had the good sense to understand her DS's mind was in overdrive.

'I'll meet you there,' she replied, and killed the call.

Nash got to the hospital and texted Moretti to advise him she'd arrived. They met outside and went to find the SOIT officer.

They found her in a side room off a main ward. She was in her twenties, brunette, hair scraped back from her forehead that was braided down to her neck. She was making notes in her SOIT log and looked up as Nash tapped on the door to the room, Moretti behind her.

'The nurses' station is down the corridor on the right,' the officer said.

'DI Nash, and this is DS Moretti, Homicide Command. You contacted the incident room?'

The officer closed the log and sat back in her chair.

'Sorry, guv. It's been a long night; I'm PC Roberts, Sonia Roberts, Sapphire. Thanks for attending so quickly and not making me come to you.'

Nash sat opposite and draped her jacket behind her.

'No problem, but don't get any ideas of handing this over to my team. You're the experts in this field, not us. It's been a long night for you, don't you have an early turn who can take this on?' Nash said.

The officer laughed.

'You haven't worked on borough for a while have you?'

Nash shrugged. 'Point taken. So, what can you tell me? How's the victim?'

'Diane's doing all right, considering the trauma she's been through. She presented last night after she'd broken down in front of her best mate who suggested she sought medical help. Her friend said she'd be better off going to hospital rather than her GP as the hospital would be more empathetic and know who to contact in the police. That's when I was called...' She paused as a nurse stuck her head into the room.

'Would either of you like a drink? I'm just making one,' the nurse said.

'I'd love a tea please,' Moretti said.

Nash and Roberts both put their orders in, and the nurse left.

'Please carry on,' Nash said.

'As I was saying, I spoke with Diane and tried to get an initial account so that I could establish what had happened, where and when. She explained that a few weeks ago she'd been returning home from work when she sensed she was being followed. She didn't look around, out of fear, and she thought her mind might have been playing tricks on her. As she got closer to the block where she lives, she was grabbed from behind and a hand was put over her mouth. She tried to kick out but was overpowered. She was forced into an alley and dragged into a bush. Her mouth was taped and her hands bound. She was raped… vaginally. She had her eyes closed for most of the assault but does remember the suspect wore a balaclava.' PC Roberts paused before she looked up from her notes.

'A few weeks ago?' Moretti asked.

'Diane is clear it was a few weeks ago. Three, at the most. She never reported it as she was in such a state of shock and didn't think she'd be believed.'

'The alleyway where it happened, where is that exactly?' Nash asked.

'It runs close to the Howard Estate not far from the posh blocks near the river like Thamesmere Heights,' PC Roberts said.

Nash listened and as Roberts finished, she thought of the proximity to the murder scenes and the rape kit in the panniers of Buchanan's motorbike. Nash's mind was working hard as she assimilated what she knew from her caseload with this additional information. A silence had fallen on the group and Roberts looked between the two detectives.

'Was it something I said?' she asked.

'I'm afraid I'll have to remain vague with you, at this time, but you've been most helpful so don't worry. You did absolutely the right thing in calling us,' Nash said. 'In the mean-time I will get your crime report restricted so that only a few who need to see it can. I trust the alley is secured as a scene?'

'Yes,' Roberts replied.

'Good. A member of my team will attend as an observer while the SOCO is there. When will Diane be spoken to?'

'Well, she's not fit at present. She took a turn after speaking with me.'

Nash produced a card and handed it to Roberts. 'When she's ready for interview I'd like to be notified. I'll need one of my team to be present in the audio room behind the one-way screen. She may, and I emphasise *may*, be able to assist us with our enquiry. However, I appreciate she's in no fit state to be spoken to and it's unclear whether we will need to,' Nash said as she stood up and grabbed her jacket from the back of the chair just as the nurse returned with the drinks.

They shook hands with Roberts and left. Nash phoned the incident room and spoke with Sagona to raise actions in relation to the event and get Jonesy down to the scene to see what was being done. He needed to be eyes and ears only while the SOCO worked. Anything of interest was to be fed back to her. She then phoned the SOIT officer's DI and appraised him of the developments.

As they got back to Moretti's car her phone went.

'Nash,' she said.

'Guv, it's the custody inspector here. Mr Buchanan is being taken to hospital, suspected heart attack after his solicitor informed him of the warrant of further detention. Thought you'd wish to know.'

Nash thanked the inspector and closed the call.

'You look flustered?' Moretti said.

'Our suspect is on route to hospital with a suspected heart attack.'

'Oh dear,' he replied, as he ducked into the car.

CHAPTER TWENTY-ONE

Buchanan was flat on his back, his head caressed by a nest of pillows. A section of blue fluff had divorced itself from the cell blanket and attached to his pillowcase. He wasn't handcuffed to the bed, but was under the watchful eye of PC Tipton, a probationer whose sole purpose was to ensure Buchanan remained in the hospital until officially released.

Buchanan awaited being seen. For Nash it gave her more time to work the investigations. Time that she could ill afford to waste.

'Penny for them?' Moretti said whilst they headed back to base.

Crossing Westminster Bridge, the traffic was as sluggish as ever. Nash stared out of the window as a pleasure boat meandered along. She restrained the desire to wave at the tourists as they enjoyed London's rich history, unaware of the brutality it harboured on a daily basis.

'Where next?'

'The office, I thought,' Moretti said.

'No, I mean where in terms of the enquiries?'

'Why not go to the CPS and get a charge authorised? God knows we have enough for Melissa Phelps. Jade Williams is certainly on the cards, even though circumstantial; if the Crown saw fit to link the two and fall on balance of probabilities.'

Nash observed the wash from the tourist boat as it swirled in a white mass of foam and water whilst she considered Moretti's suggestion. It was tempting.

'No. I don't want him to slip the net on a technicality in our rush to get him on the sheet. We need a solid case for both victims. How's Jade's scene looking?' Nash asked.

'SOCO have very little to go on. The killer's meticulously clean. Buchanan doesn't strike me as much of a neat freak when you look at the state of the garage he used. I'm not saying it should look like an advert for a cleaning firm, but it would be suggestive of a disorganised mind and our killer would appear to be anything but,' Moretti said.

Nash nodded. She liked the way he remained open-minded as to whom they sought. Her phone came to life.

'Nash,' she answered.

'Guv, it's Owen. Are you coming back to the office? I've something to show you that may open up a line of enquiry,' DS Matthews said.

'I was considering eloping with Moretti and risking my pension but now you've said that – well, I'm on my way.' She hung up.

'Charming. What makes you think I'd be interested in eloping with you? You've more baggage than a British Airways luggage hold,' Moretti said.

Nash shook her head as Moretti drove.

* * *

As they entered the incident room Nash was pleased to see phones being answered and camaraderie among her staff. Those not inside were still engaged in the day's actions. House-to-house follow-ups and CCTV were still on-going. Jonesy was out at the rape scene and hadn't called the office with any update. Despite Jonesy's maverick approach to detective duty, he was a dedicated officer and Nash was confident he'd call when he needed to.

They went to find DS Owen Matthews. He was tucked away surrounded by mobile office dividers.

'Excuse the mess, I'm in the middle of our relocation into the main incident room as you can see, but there isn't the space to occupy everything we had in this nice, secure, little room off the corridor that the canteen staff now inhabit,' he said as Moretti and Nash drew up chairs around Matthews's desk and awaited his revelation.

Nash shrugged off Matthews's resentment at giving up his office, but she'd been given no choice. Office space had become so scarce as so much property was being sold off. Hot-desking and remote working from secure laptops was now in vogue, causing a management headache at the best of times.

'Right, I've found what I need,' Matthews said, spreading various sheets of A4 across the table in front of his audience.

The pages contained pictures of cats. Nash glanced at Moretti.

'Now, I know you're thinking, what the fuck are we looking at pictures of cats for?' Matthews said. 'But there's a valid reason I assure you.' He looked about for his own seat and realised Moretti had occupied it. As one of his DCs got up to see Sagona, Matthews commandeered his.

'Remember you asked me to research social media history for each victim? Well, we did, and this is what we found...'

'A love of cats?' Moretti mocked.

'Yes and no. They both had the usual accounts: Facebook, Twitter, Snapchat. What revealed the most for our purposes was Instagram.' Matthews paused as Moretti and Nash scanned the images in front of them.

'Owen, forgive me, but none of these images are of the victims' cats? So what relevance is this to the investigation?' Nash asked.

She picked one photo up. It showed a hairless creature all pink-skinned which looked like a rat with alopecia that affected the entire body.

'They're meant to be hairless. It's a breed thing,' Matthews commented as he took back the image and replaced it in the order he'd arranged them.

'Anyway, you've thrown me off track. Now, where was I? Oh yes. Each victim loved to show where they were and what they were doing despite their high-profile roles within their own fields. They liked to get out at weekends and let their hair down. Lots of images at clubs and wine bars for Phelps, while Williams preferred restaurants and coffee places.'

'Owen – what do you want us to know that was so urgent we came in?' Nash asked.

It wasn't that she didn't value what Matthews had to say, it was that Matthews had previous for not getting to the point.

'Sorry. Each victim shot images with location services active on their phones. This meant whenever they uploaded an image to any of the sites, it was shown where and when it was taken. Naturally, they both uploaded more images to Instagram and every single shot had the location it was taken.' Matthews paused.

Nash's eyes widened, as she held her hands out, palms towards Matthews, her forearms on her thighs as she bent forward. When he didn't carry on, she spoke.

'That's interesting. Not being a fan of social media, I find it astonishing that you can do that, but how is it *relevant* to our enquiries? It's good that we can build a lifestyle picture beyond what we found at each flat. Can we link Buchanan to each scene beyond what we have at present in addition to his statement and the forensics? On the phone you sounded like you had more than that?' Nash said.

Matthews turned away from his computer screen and tapped the images on the desk that contained cats.

'You're right, Pip, none of these images contain our victims' cats, but all these cats live in the same blocks as our victims,' he said.

Before Moretti or Nash could comment, Matthews produced further pages of A4. Each sheet contained pictures of the victims' cats. Each image Matthews had captured from their Instagram sites showed the location of where the victim lived. He produced a further sheet. The data showed the images they'd taken over the period of a year. First, Melissa Phelps. Each thumbnail of her cat showed an image from kitten to adulthood. Each taken with the location displayed.

'So, these show Melissa's block as an address?' Nash asked.

'Yes. All you have to do is click on the location the image was taken and you go to a map. Zoom in and there's the block. Now, if the killer knew her Instagram account then he could work out where she lived by following her or trying other Internet searches for name and address. Same for Jade. Hers too showed her block as the location where each image of her cat was taken,' Matthews said.

He sat back and placed his arms behind his head, rocking the swivel chair with the sides of his brown leather boots as he massaged the floor.

Both Nash and Moretti remained silent for a short while as they considered the presentation. It was interesting but was it significant? The suspect could've followed each victim and established a pattern of lifestyle using the pictures of places frequented from social media pages as a resource. A possibility.

'What privacy setting is on the accounts?' Moretti asked.

'They're both private. Only those following them can see the images,' Matthews said.

Moretti stood up and went over to the murder board Matthews hated so much and looked at how it was shaping up. Pictures of the victims, and one of Buchanan on his motorbike, and his mug shot from custody, tacked to the board along with the block details for each victim and a map of where they were situated.

He turned back to Matthews.

'Correct me if I'm wrong, Owen, but are you theorising our killer is targeting cat lovers via Instagram? From the locations posted, as a result of their phone settings, he or she knows where they live?' Moretti raised his eyebrows.

Matthews ruffled his hair.

'Now you say it aloud it does sound far-fetched, but when I established the pattern it seemed feasible,' Matthews said.

'But that would mean the killer is on each of their friendship lists, wouldn't it?' Nash chipped in.

'Well, it's a possibility,' Matthews said.

Moretti sat back down.

Nash addressed Matthews, 'Check the friends list for each victim and see what you find. If Buchanan is on both, I want to know. If nothing shows, then we'll reconvene and decide whether to pursue the line of enquiry or put it to bed. Any other links with Buchanan beyond what we already know then I want to be informed. I want the same done for Buchanan with any social media sites associated to him. We'll look at the venues the victims habitually frequented and get them visited with an image of Buchanan. Let's see if he's been to any of those and asking questions. If he has, I want to know when and why he was there.'

Nash went back to her office and was greeted by a mountain of paperwork. She sat down and pulled her in tray towards her as she summoned the energy for the task ahead. Moretti knocked on her door.

'Can I come in?' he asked.

'Of course. I need a distraction from this lot,' she said, a batch of paperwork in her hand.

'I've just heard from Jonesy. They've finished at the rape scene. Jonesy made sure Dan, the SOCO, spoke with me before he left. I've told him to ensure any marks, DNA or fibres, are compared with what we found in each of our scenes. He said he'd liaise with our SOCO, Yvonne, as soon as he had any results. Jonesy mentioned the SOCO had retrieved some fibres and a partial shoe mark, but he's not certain there's enough for a match. Nevertheless, it's something and at the very least it may help catch the bastard who raped her,' he said.

Nash nodded her appreciation. If nothing came back from forensics or a witness soon, she realised the prospects of holding Buchanan for longer without charge were falling away. Time would tell and she knew too well the clock was ticking.

CHAPTER TWENTY-TWO

'Turn that off, Jonesy, it's doing my head in,' Matthews said as he palmed the steering wheel of the BMW 3 Series to pass a stationary bus. Why he was the only person who could collect Jonesy was beyond him, but he'd agreed to come out to give himself a break from his screen.

Jonesy reached for the car radio and switched to another station.

'I never got into the Beastie Boys,' Matthews commented as *Fight For Your Right* subsided and Natalie Imbruglia's *Torn* invaded the vehicle.

'That's because you're a stiff,' Jonesy retorted with a smirk, as he stared out the window at the passers-by scurrying in and out of shops like lemmings on speed.

'Whoa, look at that lot,' Jonesy remarked. He nodded in the direction of a trio of mopeds. All were being ridden two-up and moved as though they were the only ones on the road.

'They're gonna do a job, Owen, I can feel it and we're going to take the fuckers out.' Jonesy unclicked his seatbelt.

'Jonesy, put your belt back on,' Matthews said as Jonesy's keen eyes followed the riders' paths. All three mopeds now cruised in a V formation.

'Over there, they're scoping that phone shop,' Jonesy said, his voice rose in pitch as his adrenaline built.

'I've a mate in the Flying Squad who'd give his right arm to be in my seat now,' he continued.

Matthews decreased the pressure on the accelerator, and they dropped back from the trio of bikes while he connected his phone. They had no radio, and neither of them would know which channel to select if they did for the area of London they were in. What Matthews did know was that Holborn station was close by. Matthews banged in three nines and asked for police.

'Police operator. What's the nature of your call?'

'DS Matthews, Homicide Command. I'm in Holborn and I believe there's about to be an armed robbery of a phone shop on Theobalds Road.'

'How do you know this?' the operator asked.

Matthews paused. Outside, his view had changed from one of flowing traffic to stationary vehicles. Screams from pedestrians erupted as the mopeds mounted the pavement. The rear passengers were off the bikes before they'd stopped, and began to stove in the shop window with a sledgehammer, while one rider remained roadside and threatened anyone who got close with a hammer.

Matthews turned towards Jonesy. The passenger door was open and his seat vacant. He returned to his call.

'I know because they're smashing the place up with a hammer and I have a DC who's bailed out of my car towards them. Urgent assistance.'

Matthews dropped the line and looked over to the shop. Jonesy was closer to the group as he weaved between cars that had come to a standstill in the street. People had congregated, their phones held aloft as though a royal had been spotted. No one attempted to intervene. The only heroic act for them was being the first to get the footage uploaded to social media. Some jostled for the best position in the effort to achieve the status.

Jonesy waited by the rear of a parked car. He was close enough to the robbers to observe and evaluate a tactic of approach. He could either react, or stay and gather as much evidence as he could through observation. He had no radio and hoped backup was on its way. The robbers weren't paying him any attention as they loaded the stolen goods into backpacks they carried. One of them who'd entered the shop was now back out and screamed for his cohorts to go. His voice loud but muffled through the helmet's visor that was pulled down over his face. Jonesy heard the sound of distant sirens and hoped they were police and not ambulance.

The mopeds' engines revved in readiness to abscond. It was now or never. Jonesy lowered his head and took a deep breath. His heart beat a powerful rhythm as the noise around him filtered out. The only noise he was in communication with was the recognition of his own breath. He went into the inner pocket of his jacket, pulled out his ASP, and racked it open in one fluid motion.

Matthews saw Jonesy rise from his position of safety behind a parked car, ASP held aloft. Matthews froze. His mind raced as he considered what to do. He saw a gap in the traffic that had been created by one of the mopeds in order for them to disperse. He reached over and shut the passenger door, selected sport mode on the auto gearbox and floored the accelerator. Matthews watched as Jonesy stealthily approached a rider. Matthews saw that the pillion that'd entered the shop had turned and seen Jonesy. The robber was reaching inside his loose jacket. Palm down, the back of his hand towards Matthews.

DS Owen Matthews formed an honestly held belief that the suspect had a gun, and that his colleague and members of the public were at risk of serious harm. Without hesitation he slammed on the horn and mounted the pavement. Jonesy turned at hearing the increased revs of an engine, and on seeing the BMW hurtle towards him, he instinctively dived out the way of the oncoming car as Matthews smashed the BMW into the side of the moped. He only stopped once the bike was pinned against the shop wall, along with the rider and pillion who were now under it.

Matthews racked the gearbox into reverse and shouted through the open passenger window at Jonesy, 'Gun!'

Jonesy heard the word, as did the public at the scene. Some screamed as others carried on recording. The two remaining moped riders were away on their rides.

Matthews leaned forward and peered through the windscreen as he looked at the end of the bonnet. He was far enough back but kept the engine running, fully prepared to do the same thing again should either rider move or attempt to get up. The two riders had started shouting abuse at each other as they lay dazed under the moped, visors up.

A high and low pitch bounced off the surrounding buildings in a cacophony of sound. All at different speeds and tones. Matthews sat with his hands at the ten-to-two position on the steering wheel. His legs were shaking. Within minutes, armed officers swarmed all over the street like bees in defence of the hive. There was a tap on Matthews's window and an armed officer stood, her MP5 levelled at his torso, as she demanded Matthews slowly turn off the engine and not make any sudden movement.

Matthews did as directed, which was easy as he was pinned by the airbag that had inflated on impact with the moped. Once the car was dead, he felt the driver's door open. His arms were grabbed, the bag dealt with, and he was dragged from the vehicle and forced to lay face down on the tarmac. Matthews knew it was coming, but as it happened he felt as though the world had slowed, like he was watching a film he was the main lead in. None of the armed officers knew he was police. He could have been part of the gang for all they knew. Safety first. Questions later.

Matthews heard Jonesy shout that Matthews was with him and as the words resonated with the officers, Matthews felt the weight upon his back relax. His wrists were dropped from the gooseneck position they'd been placed in and he was lifted to standing. As his brain adjusted to the surroundings, his eyes took in the wave of blue lights. His ears had adjusted to the sirens' call to arms. They slowly faded to silence as officers switched them off now everyone was contained.

Jonesy was by his side now. His warrant card tucked into the top of his trousers; the metal of the badge winked in the sun that had appeared over the tops of the buildings.

'Are you OK, Owen? Fuck me, that was awesome what you did there! Those two fuckers didn't know what hit 'em! Way more effective than my ASP, that's for sure,' Jonesy said as he surveyed the front of their BMW and nodded to himself in appreciation of the resulting damage.

'We'll need a lift back. Shall I call Moretti?' Jonesy said.

He didn't know if Matthews had heard him, or was just ignoring him.

The firearms officer who was with Matthews was astute enough to have Matthews sit back in her car.

'Did you find a gun?' Matthews quietly asked.

'I don't think so, but I could be wrong. I wasn't controlling the suspects. They're both alive though,' she said.

Matthews remained silent as a member of the London Ambulance Service joined them. She professionally brushed the firearms officer aside and crouched down level with Matthews's face.

'Haven't we been in the wars then?' she said as she gloved up and pressed lightly on Matthews's forehead.

'Ouch!' he responded.

'I'm not surprised it hurts. You've had quite a knock there. Your head must have hit part of the car before the airbag went off. I'm surprised one of your colleagues hadn't told you?'

Matthews looked at Jonesy.

'Sorry, Owen. I was too stoked at the result we've had,' Jonesy replied.

'Result? Jonesy, it's a fucking mess – sorry,' Matthews said to the ambulance officer.

'No need to apologise. I've heard worse and you are in shock. Not that I need to tell you your job, but I'd say nothing until you've been seen by a doctor,' she told him.

'Really?' Jonesy asked.

'Yes. My other half is in the police and he asked me to pass the advice on should I attend an incident such as this that involved police. For at least twenty-four hours, anyway. Your brain is in survival mode at the moment and may mislead your recollection of events. Now, let's get you checked out at hospital,' she said, as she got up.

'Hospital? I'm fine, really, I am. Just need a sweet cup of tea and I'm good to go,' Matthews said.

Jonesy stepped closer to Matthews, who was still sitting in the car and dropped to his level so he could see his face clearly.

'Look, Sarge, what you did probably saved my life. I didn't think about a gun until you raised the question a minute ago. Now, let's say they didn't have one, you need some space to think and get your head together because we know who'll be all over this like a granny at a tabletop sale,' Jonesy said, placing a hand on Matthews's shoulder.

Matthews looked up and held a hand to his forehead to shield his eyes from the sun. As he did a shadow appeared behind Jonesy. It wasn't the typical outline of a firearms officer.

'That would be me then,' a low, Glaswegian voice said.

The shadow stepped into a better position for Matthews and Jonesy to see. He was five-eight, his gut strained against his taut leather belt. He sported a moustache that would've looked good on a hipster, but on him appeared like he'd walked into a hedge and collected a long-haired caterpillar on the way back out. He snapped his warrant card open with a rehearsed flick of his wrist.

'DI Richards, Professional Standards. I'm the first responder for incidents such as these that involve police, collisions and injured members of the public,' the man said.

'Members of the public? No one was injured!' Jonesy said.

'That's not the impression I was given when I saw the two males under the moped.'

'Do me a favour,' Jonesy said as he stood up and stepped towards Richards.

Richards stood his ground, hands in his pockets.

'DC Jones, I believe? I would advise you to calm down and see the situation from my point of view and the public's. An incident such as this where police have rammed into another human being on a pedestrian footway can't be ignored. It's already on social media sites and getting a lot of attention. Go and get seen by the LAS, too. You must be in shock yourself after what you witnessed. I'm not an idiot, detectives, and can see the situation. Now help me to help you.'

With that, Richards walked away to join other suited and booted colleagues of his who'd arrived on scene. Matthews stood up and the ambulance officer helped him. Jonesy took Matthews's arm as his legs began to shake as though he was stuck on a cliff edge with no more hand or foot holds to speak of. Since the arrival of DI Richards neither had noticed the LAS woman had produced an ambulance chair. A chair Matthews was now lowered onto. As Matthews was pirouetted towards the awaiting ambulance, he turned his head towards his right shoulder. 'Jonesy,' he beckoned.

'Yeah.'

'As you're the fleet manager, you can call Nash and give her the good news she's a car down,' Matthews said as he was pushed towards the back doors of the ambulance.

'Great, just great. Even in a concussed state, you're still an arsehole,' Jonesy replied with a smile that Matthews weakly returned.

CHAPTER TWENTY-THREE

Nash put down the receiver on her desk phone and looked up at the square ceiling tiles of her office. Jonesy had explained the events he and Matthews had been involved in. She was relieved that they were both alive and relatively unscathed. She got up from behind her desk and shouted across the corridor for Moretti to join her.

'What's up with you? Please tell me we haven't copped another murder, making it three?' he said.

Moretti took a seat in her office. Nash swept some papers from her desk and perched on the edge.

'Jonesy and Matthews took out an armed robbery team on their way back. All of the robbers were on mopeds. Two down – them, not us – both in hospital with non-life-threatening injuries. Our BMW's written off though. Matthews took a bang to the head and Jonesy – well, Jonesy's Jonesy. He walked away, thankfully,' she explained.

Moretti took out his phone and brought up YouTube. He searched for *police + mopeds – London.*

'Here it is,' he said.

He got up and joined Nash at her desk. They watched the scene unravel, courtesy of a person known as Dubz. It was a short clip but captured all they needed to see. Nash stood and placed her hands in her pockets. She thought through what could have happened to both her officers had the scene played out differently.

'Jonesy told me Matthews reacted in the way he did because he thought one of the suspects had a gun. I just hope that's the case. If it isn't, he still did the right thing in my mind. They both deserve a commendation for the actions they took. Anyway, we now have quite a gathering at St Thomas's Hospital,' Nash declared. 'I'll go to the hospital and see them. I need you here co-ordinating the murder investigations while I ensure Matthews and Jonesy are being looked after. I'll let Matthews's wife know too and arrange a car should she wish to go and see him at the hospital.' She grabbed her coat from a hook on the back of her door.

Moretti sat at Nash's desk.

'Don't mind if I use your office for a while do you? I want to run through what Matthews came up with on the social media side. I think we came across as dismissive of his work,' he said.

* * *

Nash found her car, pressed the fob and the indicators winked yellow. She got in and fired up the engine. While the engine warmed, she took out her work phone and scrolled through the numbers. She found Harris and dialled. It was answered after three tones.

'Pip, always a pleasure,' Harris said.

'Not today it isn't. I have two of mine in hospital as a result of those shits on mopeds who rob phone shops. Two were nicked and four fled the scene on two mopeds and are now at large.' She paused to afford Harris time to digest the information.

She could hear him scrabbling around as though he was looking for something. She surmised it must be a pen and some paper he sought. His attention was back with her.

'Sorry to hear that, Pip. It goes without saying, if anything comes across our work then you will be the first to know. You know me, I'm old school where our own are concerned. Rest assured, I'll be focussed on anything discussed in the sting shop, or property presented that links to the robbery,' Harris said.

'That's what I needed to hear. Now, here's what I know so far…' Nash said and explained what she'd ascertained.

Moretti laid out the phone data along with the Instagram images. He was a stickler for privacy and although he used social media, he was under a pseudonym with the highest privacy settings that he kept refreshed as often as his mind reminded him. He also knew it wouldn't take a determined person long to work out who he was through his friends who weren't as security conscious as him. Detection by association.

Melissa and Jade had a similar number of friends listed and were clearly focussed on people they knew rather than those they didn't. Between them they had four hundred friends. The accounts were clearly a way of sharing their lives with people they trusted and felt comfortable with seeing their images. Both victims were iPhone users, which helped Moretti concentrate on the one operating system. He clicked on Melissa's profile page and then the location symbol. A map sprang up that showed a large concentration of photos in one area. As he clicked over the area, it identified Melissa's block.

As each image was clicked, it showed her cat. He right-clicked on one of the photos, and up came the EXIF data. Data that showed everything about the photo, from picture size and camera settings to the time it was taken and where.

He expanded the size of the font and what he saw made him sit back as he stared at the phone. Initially he thought it was a fluke but on every picture over her block it showed a time. Each image had been taken on a weekday at about 6:45 p.m. Moretti knew he didn't have the time to go through each image. He gathered up the paperwork and went through to the Intelligence Section.

There was a solemn air about cosy corner. The section was usually active and upbeat. Matthews enjoyed having background music playing and this was absent.

Sally Clarke was a member of police staff – a demure girl in her twenties who kept herself to herself and was more than happy to be occupied with a computer-based task, as long as she could wear her headphones and listen to her choice of music. She wasn't a fan of eye contact, and when Moretti had first arrived on the unit, he'd queried with Nash why she had recruited such a rude member of staff who barely spoke and couldn't possibly answer a phone if she wore headphones.

Nash had explained that she'd been sent on an autism awareness training day with an outside agency. She'd come away having enjoyed a free lunch and coffee on tap and, when it was over, she'd stayed and discussed her need for an analyst on her Intel desk with the organiser of the event.

Nash had left her card and forwarded an application form to the person in the agency who'd organised the event. Clarke applied. She'd been there for over a year. She'd never been sick, did her allotted hours and more, when required, and always completed a task on time. Where identifying, extracting and linking data was concerned, she was the go-to person.

Moretti noticed Clarke had seen him out the corner of her eye. He waited for her to finish what she was doing and remove her headphones. He sat beside her and explained what was required.

'Will Sergeant Matthews be all right?' she asked as she placed the paperwork in a tray and ensured the base of each A4 sheet aligned evenly as she listened.

'Yes, he should be fine. He's in hospital to make sure he's fit to go home and then, hopefully, back here with you,' he said.

'Hopefully?' Clarke asked.

'Just an expression, a poor one really,' he said.

'He wants to go on holiday.'

'Does he? He never mentioned that to me. I would have covered for him,' Moretti said.

'He knows there's no holiday time while people keep getting stiffed – his words not mine. He also said he'd look at the social media accounts for the victims as I was up to my eyes in work. I tried to explain the level of my in tray was no higher than my chin, but he just smiled and got on with it. I knew he hadn't done it right,' she said.

Moretti went to give her a reassuring touch on the arm but stopped himself, smiled and left. She had already attached her headphones and was engrossed in the first sheet as Moretti glanced back at her. Clarke was right. A holiday is what they all needed. He got back to his desk just as his desk phone began to blink indicating an active call.

He picked up.

'Is DI Nash there please?' a female voice enquired.

'No, I'm afraid not,' he said.

'It's the ward sister at St Thomas's Hospital, I need to speak to her urgently.'

'Can I help? It's DS Moretti. DI Nash is on her way to you as we speak,' Moretti said.

'My, that's quick. I've only just found out Mr Buchanan has left the building... hello?'

Moretti dropped the phone back in its cradle and grabbed his jacket and car keys. The last thing to be heard was the vibration of the handrail on the stairs as he bounded down each flight and out of the building towards his vehicle.

CHAPTER TWENTY-FOUR

Nash stopped pacing the small side room of the hospital and took a deep breath. PC Tipton sat, hat in hands as he turned it over. He explained the circumstances that had led to Buchanan absconding. Tipton had needed a leak and a nurse offered to sit with Buchanan while he went. That nurse was now being treated for a puncture wound to the back of his neck, after Buchanan had plunged a biro he'd secreted under the mattress into the soft tissue at the base of the nurse's skull.

'I've radioed in and units are out searching for him. I'm sorry, boss,' Tipton said, as he waited for Nash to admonish him.

A minute can seem like an eternity when you're expecting the worst. Nash turned to him.

'Just get out there and find him,' she said.

Tipton sullenly placed his flat hat on his head and closed the door on his way out.

There was a light knock and Nash turned towards the sound as Moretti entered.

'Thank God,' she said.

'I've been referred to as worse. I take it the PC I just saw dragging his sorry arse was Group Four's next recruit?'

'The very same.'

'I've updated George on the developments, and Buchanan's details and description are now circulated to all cars.'

'So, how's things with Matthews and Jonesy?'

'They're out searching,' she said.

'Bloody hell, they're like Batman and Robin. Are they OK?'

'The doctor said they're both fine and recommended a day's recovery before being interviewed, which I will ensure is adhered to once they return. I hope they find Buchanan soon, Nick. If he's our man and kills again…'

'Let's not go there. I'm certain he'll come to notice. He's dressed in a hospital gown and no shoes. He won't get far,' Moretti said with a note of reassurance.

Nash didn't have Moretti's faith in the crippled system. Due to the cuts and lack of officers, they were lucky to get a copper to be on a hospital watch such was the shortfall on the streets.

Moretti could tell Nash was downbeat. He explained what he'd done back at the incident room in the hope it would lift her mood.

'I've got Sally reviewing Matthews's Instagram work. I had a look myself and discovered a pattern to the times the cat images were taken. All were taken on or around 6:45 p.m. If the killer's on her friends list then they'd soon work out she'd be in at that time. If, and it's a big if, Buchanan has access to her account, then we should know pretty soon. Sally's good and if it's there, she'll find it and make it stand in court,' Moretti said.

'That's good to know. At least we'll get a fast result if she finds anything. I need him in custody more than ever now, he's a liability and if he isn't guilty, he's not making a good case of convincing me to look elsewhere.'

The blur of a dark coat flashed past the glass in the room's door. They had both been affected by the brief change in light and were looking at the door as it burst open.

Jonesy was bent over, out of breath, and as Nash went towards him to help, he extended his left arm, palm out.

'I'm OK, just a bit fucked from running all over the hospital trying to find you both.' He paused to get his breath then continued, 'We've found him – Buchanan.'

CHAPTER TWENTY-FIVE

'What's the situation?' Nash asked.

Matthews was busy ushering staff and patients along the corridor and away from the main ward.

'Buchanan is in the side room with a woman. He's got hold of a scalpel and holding her at knife point. He's demanded some clothes and to be let out of the building. He wants a taxi and once he's in it, he says he'll let her go. He wants no police outside. If he sees any, he'll kill her,' Matthews said.

As he spoke, a porter rushed by with a patient on a trolley being evacuated from the main ward. As the ward door swung open a figure caught Nash's eye.

'Owen, who's that female? The one not in nurse's uniform near the main desk area?'

'I don't know. She was with the woman in the room according to the ward sister, but she couldn't tell me more as she was trying to calm everyone down and get people away,' Matthews said.

It suddenly dawned on Nash who she was, and everything fell into place. It was PC Sonia Roberts, the SOIT officer she'd seen earlier. Nash moved closer to the door and peered through the ward window.

'Oh no – he's got Diane in there,' she said.

'Diane?' Matthews asked.

Moretti was by Nash's side now. He could see PC Roberts standing with both palms held out as she spoke towards the open door of the room where Diane was being held.

'Diane is the victim of rape from the scene Jonesy attended,' Nash said to Matthews.

Matthews turned and rested his forehead against the wall. He then stood back and faced them again.

'Can this day get any worse?' he said as a uniform inspector joined them. He had been called by the hospital security once Buchanan had been discovered missing.

'Is one of you DI Nash?' he asked.

Nash turned at hearing her name.

'That would be me,' she said with an air of despair as she looked at the imposing figure before her.

'Inspector Dylan Ivers. I'm the duty inspector as well as a hostage negotiator. I understand you know all about the time sapper who's about to ruin my meal plans later,' he said.

Nash nodded her sympathies.

'So, what can you tell me about him before I try and build a rapport?' Ivers asked as he removed his black clip-on tie and placed it in his flat hat.

'All I can tell you is that he's a ticking bomb. As well as being a suspect for two murders, there's a charge of rape and a new rape investigation. He's managed to be brought to the same hospital as his potential victim. The only bonus is I don't believe he's made the connection yet,' Nash replied as she peered, side-on, through the glass in the door to the ward.

'So, pretty straightforward then,' Ivers replied, peering over Nash's shoulder through the window. 'At least I know one of them in there.' Ivers nodded in the direction of PC Roberts who was sat side-on to them, balanced on the edge of the nurses' station.

'Well, you can leave now. There's plenty for you to be doing and he's secure. I have other officers in the hospital. I'll keep you updated and let you know when your suspect is returning to his cell. I've spoken with the doctor in charge of his care and she wants him out of here as quickly as possible. It would appear your man's a good actor. They'd conducted some tests when he bailed and there's nothing adverse with his heart,' Ivers said as he left to find a phone.

Nash extracted herself from the doorway. Behind her Moretti, Matthews and Jonesy were sat on a bench. All looked exhausted. Nash strolled over to them.

'Another fine mess,' she said.

Moretti looked up from his phone and Jonesy and Matthews remained in repose, legs out, arms folded across their chests, heads drooped, eyes closed.

'Let's get the hell out of here,' Nash said, rousing the two sleeping policemen.

* * *

Nash brought the team to attention. All staff were present other than Jonesy, Matthews and Moretti. Moretti was with Clarke outside the room. They'd dropped Matthews and Jonesy at their respective homes from hospital. Nash didn't want them anywhere near the incident room as one sniff of them being available to talk and DI Richards of Professional Standards would have them in an interview room quicker than Buchanan could abscond from a ward.

'Thanks for getting back here so quickly. I'm aware you are all busy. I'll keep this update as brief as I can,' Nash said.

The others in the room shifted to a comfortable position.

'So far the investigations haven't moved as quickly as we would've liked.'

Murmurs of agreement echoed around the table.

'However, we can only go where the evidence takes us. So far that's been scant. What we can say is that Buchanan was in Melissa's flat. We have the physical evidence and also his prepared statement. What we can't say is that he killed Melissa or knew or had any contact with Jade.

'We also know that he used a garage belonging to his girlfriend,' she continued. 'In that garage was a set of motorbike panniers that contained what can be described as a rape kit. The contents are all being forensically examined. In addition to the rape, we await the results to see if any item can be linked to Melissa or Jade.'

'I thought Dr King found no signs of sexual interference at each scene,' a young DC from the outside team queried.

'That's right. But that's not to say our victims haven't encountered Buchanan before and for whatever reason failed to report a rape or attempted rape. We can't ask them now, and we need to close that door so the defence can't argue that he had but didn't murder them. As far as we can ascertain, Buchanan had done some work for Melissa on her bathroom. He's acknowledged as much in a prepared statement. As for Jade, we don't know yet. The only person he's admitted seeing, but not touching, is Melissa when he saw her in the bath and was already dead,' Nash answered.

'In addition, we have a victim of rape who's entered the investigation albeit on the periphery. Our team won't be investigating her allegation, but the MO would fit with Buchanan's previous in relation to the charge of rape he's wanted for. The SOIT officer thought the same and made contact as a result of the Intranet appeal. Unfortunately, the victim's now a hostage of Buchanan at St Thomas's Hospital, so if he's the suspect for that rape then that investigative team have a huge mountain to climb. It's not insurmountable as far as forensic transfer goes,' she said.

Her heart felt heavy. She looked at the sea of faces, most sported shadows under their eyes.

'Buchanan isn't going to walk away from this. He will go back inside, but I want him to remain there until he dies. I want him to receive multiple charges, but unless we can come up with anything more concrete, he will walk at court on our murders,' Nash said.

As she looked around the table, she was aware that Clarke wasn't there. This wasn't unusual. Matthews would always relay anything she had established, and Nash would follow up outside the meeting.

'I have something from the Intelligence Desk,' Moretti said as he entered the room and held a file aloft.

There were a few sniggers at the suggestion the Intelligence Desk had come up with anything worthwhile and Moretti knew they'd soon be sitting mouths agape once he'd fed back the results.

'I'm sorry to intrude like this, guv, but it's important,' he said.

Now he'd announced this, ears were pricked. Nash smiled and Moretti sat down and passed a copy of the file along the table eventually arriving to Nash.

'DS Matthews had been looking at the social media accounts for the victims. He had proposed a theory that the killer may be connected with each victim via their friends list, as they had access to the images posted. Some of which were marked with where they were taken. He thought this could be a lead, as the killer would know where they lived and hence where he'd strike. However, I reallocated this to Sally once DS Matthews became indisposed, and she's worked on the Instagram account for each victim,' Moretti said.

He opened the file and handed out sheets of A4 around the table.

The sheets showed images of cats and a map of where they were taken. Another showed a timeline of when they were taken.

'I wasn't convinced by the theory that the killer was a friend of either victim from what Matthews had suggested. Mainly because these women were cautious about whom they associated with. Despite going out socially, they didn't just add anyone they met to their social media accounts. Each account was private, but they hadn't disabled location services on their phones and the app was enabled for this service. However, you couldn't see Melissa or Jade's pictures unless you were added as a friend.' Moretti paused, as he attempted to recall how Clarke had explained everything to him. It had to be Moretti who relayed the information because she found talking to the DCs exasperating –what was common sense to her was at times like another language to the officers.

'So, where does this take us?' Moretti continued. 'Sally had access to the accounts and could work on the images. She's extracted what's known as EXIF data for each picture and this is shown against a selection of the photos. As you will see, the pictures were taken at the same time on the same day of each week. The time is around 6:45 p.m.'

'I don't understand how this helps?' Sagona said.

This was met with nods of agreement around the room.

Moretti continued, 'A friends list for both Melissa and Jade is small by comparison to most. None are connected between the victims or have any connection to Buchanan. Sally has also looked at Buchanan's phone. He's on Facebook only but under a pseudonym. Sally was able to establish the pseudonym was Buchanan's by his associates, places frequented, and music and film tastes. It's not difficult and when you look at how she did it, it becomes clear. It's hard to remain anonymous on social media when your associates don't. Truth gets added in images and posts and that leads to identity revelation.'

Sagona raised his pen like a kid at school.

'So, if it isn't taking us anywhere, we can now put this to bed and concentrate on another area that will provide a lead?' Sagona said. It sounded like he was still upset at the linked cases and the volume of work he had on the go.

Moretti smirked and waved his chewed pen in his direction.

'Less haste, our Keeper of the Gates. Sally looked at the phone data for the victims' incoming and outgoing calls and she noticed a number that appeared once, calling out and coming in. The significance of the number was that it showed on both victims' call data.'

Nash stopped writing and looked up at Moretti.

'It's a non-attributable number, but CRIMINT shows a log that's marked as protected for your eyes only, ma'am,' he said with a frown.

Nash sat back, wide-eyed. The team had all turned in her direction and waited on her response.

CHAPTER TWENTY-SIX

Inspector Ivers regretted any thought he'd had on starting his shift that it would go smoothly. He'd decided to enter the ward but remain away from the side room Buchanan inhabited along with his unwilling tenant. PC Roberts remained where she was, perched on the nurses' desk, and appeared to be doing her job well – keeping Buchanan calm and his knife hand steady.

The ward was theirs. Ivers began a breathing exercise in preparation for his role. A role he'd been specially trained for. Weeks of training: sleep deprivation, talking, learning and psychological challenges under extreme pressure were about to be put into practice again. The last deployment hadn't gone as he'd hoped but he placed that at the back of his mind as he focussed on PC Roberts. This wasn't a case of good cop bad cop. Ivers didn't fit any type other than unpredictable.

Ivers waited until Buchanan became weary of the inactivity and voiced his demands. Ivers had been writing in Sharpie on A4 with instructions for PC Roberts. He held these up whenever she reached for a drink of water in a bottle that sat next to her. She could naturally look away from Buchanan without him questioning her. Ivers had written words of encouragement to reassure Roberts she was doing well, but now he needed to change tactic. He prompted her to allude she was unable to promise anything Buchanan demanded but that she'd get someone here who could. Now was her chance to introduce not only the last line of defence, but also her ticket off the ward.

'Mr Buchanan, I can't give you what you want as it's not my gift to give. I do have someone here who can listen to you though. He's also a police officer and is of a rank that can get things moving,' she said.

'Who?' Buchanan demanded.

'He's an inspector who's specially trained to help people like you.'

'What do you mean people like me? Scum, pondlife…?'

'People who mustn't be ignored,' she replied.

Ivers nodded to himself at the line and filed it for future use, and inclusion in a commendation report he intended to write for PC Roberts's benefit.

'Would you like to meet him?' she asked.

'No, fuck him. You're all right and that's good enough for me. I don't reckon anyone can ignore you when I'm stood here with this bird and a scalpel. A taxi must be here in an hour or I start carving. We're in a hospital so she might get lucky, but let me tell you, I'm fucking swift when I have a blade and know where to cut to end things quick,' Buchanan said.

Diane's muffled breathing increased in volume. Buchanan left his hand across her mouth as he drew her body closer into his. Diane felt how much he was enjoying the show and made a decision not to move for fear he'd enjoy that too.

Ivers had heard enough and stepped up to the desk where PC Roberts sat. He wore a white shirt with dark epaulettes on the shoulder that supported two pips as they were known. Enough to reassure Buchanan he was police and of rank, but not enough to scare him.

'Where'd you come from?' Buchanan barked as he stepped back from the open door to the room, taking Diane with him – the scalpel held close to her throat.

Ivers took a deep breath and prayed it wouldn't puncture her skin.

'Easy, Mr Buchanan. I'm here to help you as this officer said. PC Roberts needs a break. She's been here for some time now and she deserves a drink at least. Would you like a drink, Mr Buchanan?' Ivers asked.

'Yeah, yeah, I would. A tea. Don't think about putting any drugs in it as she'll be tasting it first,' Buchanan said, nodding at Diane.

He sat down on the edge of a hospital bed and maintained his hold of Diane. Diane squeezed her eyes shut and tried to remain as calm as she could, thankful that Buchanan was sat back enough that her bottom rested on the edge of the mattress, and not against him. She focussed on her breathing as PC Roberts had suggested they all do. Buchanan was having none of it, but PC Roberts had succeeded in calming Diane's mind as much as was possible, given the circumstances. Ivers continued.

'I'm going to let the officer leave and I will have some drinks brought in,' Ivers said.

'No. The copper gets them and comes back. If she's not back here in five minutes then it's game over,' Buchanan said.

Ivers had expected as much and was glad of the suggestion Buchanan made, as was Roberts. She got off the desk slowly and walked towards the door to the ward and left. The doors shut and remained unlocked behind her. Hospital security had overridden the electronic door lock.

Roberts rotated her neck and massaged the back of it as she left. She became aware of a weakness in her legs and rested against a wall. She bent over and placed her hands against her aching quadricep muscles as she massaged them and made the most of the limited time she had before going back in. Back in. She wished the thought hadn't arisen. She knew it was her job and that she would return with the drinks and re-enter the ward, but she felt so drained from lack of sleep she hoped she'd remain of use. She thought of Diane and that was enough to invigorate her.

A nurse approached and took her by the arm. She led her around the corner into the corridor that was eerily empty. Roberts realised the disruption Buchanan was causing to peoples' lives. An entire ward had been shut down and patients reallocated to corridors a floor up, as there wasn't the space anywhere else. This gave her a second wind and a determination to go back and wrap this up, so treatment could continue, and the hospital could return to normal and Diane could get the care she needed.

The nurse directed her to a staff room and as she entered, Roberts felt like she'd been transported to a military headquarters. Armed officers clustered in groups as they looked at maps of the ward and the entire wing of the hospital. Others ate and drank. As she entered, they all stopped what they were engaged in and turned to face her. One officer got up and passed Roberts his seat.

'He wants tea,' she said. 'I don't have long to bring it back or he'll react.'

The same officer that had offered the seat left and went to a large hot water urn and began dispensing teabags into four cups. He placed these on a tray along with milk, sugar and a plastic spoon. He handed Roberts a chocolate protein bar from a fabric lunch bag on the table.

'Here, you need this more than me. Teas are all good to go. Eat this first. The inspector will keep matey busy for a bit,' he said.

Roberts smiled, but got up and took the bar. She collected the tray, and the door was held open for her to leave. There were no questions as to how the situation was unfolding and she reached the ward door as quickly as she could.

CHAPTER TWENTY-SEVEN

'Sorry to throw a curve ball into the arena, Pip, but it seemed like an ideal opportunity,' Moretti said.

He sat on the two-seater sofa in her office while Nash moved steadily from side to side in her chair, rattling a pen in her teeth and looking at the protected CRIMINT log Moretti had uncovered. Nash knew exactly what the number pertained to. It was one she'd bought from the mobile phone shop for another operation with DS Harris's mob. She couldn't disclose to Moretti what the operation was, but it was all above board.

'So, Sally manages to find this number that's associated to me, on both victims' phone data?' Nash asked.

'Exactly. Do you recognise it?'

'Yes. It's from another UC job. I bought it from the phone shop I always use,' she mused.

'So how do you think it's ended up on both victims' call data?' Moretti asked.

'That's the million-dollar question, Nick, as neither of the victims have been associated with my work until now.'

Nash put the printout down. She'd looked at the intelligence log on the CRIMINT system. It had revealed nothing out of the ordinary. She'd put the phone number on a secure server that only she could see and access. All done in the knowledge the intelligence log would flag up if the telephone number was ever searched as well as for disclosure. She'd protectively marked it as sensitive so it wouldn't be disclosed if it was ever asked for, unless a judge said so. The operation the number related to and its purpose was classified.

Moretti watched as Nash sat in thought. He assumed she was working out how this number was coming into their investigations. Nash wasn't coming up with anything. Moretti was left with a dilemma. He trusted her but he had a duty of care to the victims and their families, and to see that justice was done. Regardless of Nash's covert work, she had to account for this anomaly. There was no question of burying it under the auspices of sensitive intelligence. A number associated to her had been used to call both their victims and she was denying it was her who'd called. A number she'd acknowledged from the intelligence entry was hers and was so sensitive the log entry couldn't be read by anyone other than her.

'What about the SIM card, Pip?'

Nash snapped out of her thoughts as Moretti fired the question.

'What about it?' she replied, rather tersely. She hadn't intended to but that's how she came across.

'Hey, don't get the arse with me. This is serious shit, and we need to bottom it out,' he said.

Moretti rubbed his face in his palms and sat back in his chair, legs out, arms behind his head as he cradled his skull. Nash sat with her head in her hands and looked up at him, her fingers gradually coming away from her hair and across her face as she sat back.

'Sorry, I'm as confused as you are and was deep in thought when you spoke,' she said. 'I bought both the phone and the SIM card from the same phone shop. It would've been one of the first times I used the place though, looking at the date of the operation I purchased the setup for. I'll draw up an action for me to establish that.'

'You?'

'Yes, me.'

'Do you think that's ethical in the circumstances?'

Nash leaned forward, her eyes wide at Moretti's assertion.

'I don't like what you're implying, Nick. You may not like my covert role or approve of undercover operations as is obvious from your lack of interaction with the source unit, but if you're hinting at corruption then you're way out of line,' Nash said.

Nash remained unflustered. Moretti had expected her reaction to be this. She had a volatile streak that surfaced at any hint of injustice and especially when it involved her team. He knew that was why she'd sent Matthews and Jonesy home. She wanted them to be out of touch from DI Richards for as long as she could engineer. For no other reason than she knew her team better than Richards, and she wanted to afford them time to account for their actions with honesty, having been given space away from a police environment to reflect and assimilate what must have been a fast-moving scene.

Moretti nodded at her and got up. There was nothing to be gained by remaining in her office. He had work to do and she most definitely did. He left her to her own mind, returned to his desk, and awaited the questions and opinions that he knew would soon fly around the room.

CHAPTER TWENTY-EIGHT

Iver's head turned as the swing doors to the ward opened and PC Roberts swayed in with the tray in an effort to ensure she didn't slop any of the teas. Her hands displayed a slight tremor and this reflected a lack of sleep and sugar. She had no fear of the situation. It was all under control. She was old enough in service to realise once a negotiator arrived, the hostage taker was either turning themselves in or being carried out covered in a black bag. Either suited her as long as she could see it through and Diane would recover from the ordeal.

Ivers helped her with the last stage of the tray's carriage. He placed it on an area of the desk he'd cleared in anticipation of its arrival. He glanced over at Buchanan who had his eye on the prize that Ivers had no intention of giving up without a fight. If Buchanan wanted it, he could come and get it – or even better, send Diane. Even Ivers knew that thought was never going to occur but it didn't do him any harm considering it as an option. An option he put in his back pocket as Buchanan pressed the blade against her throat and nodded his haggard face at the tray.

'Bring it in here and place it on the floor. If you try anything stupid, she dies,' Buchanan said. He raised his chin in Ivers's direction and licked his lower lip in anticipation of the brew.

Ivers wiped his hand over his bald head and then down the front of his trousers. The heat on the ward was becoming oppressive but he'd decided that he'd use it to his advantage. If he was feeling the heat then Buchanan was too. Ivers remained seated as he addressed his adversary.

'Can I not have a sip of mine first? It's been a testing morning already and I've got a slaker on,' he taunted as he reached for the tea.

Buchanan's eyes squeezed tight and Diane breathed in deeply as she felt Buchanan's body react to the absurdity of the response from Ivers.

'Bring the fucking drinks in here now! This is my show and the sooner you start acting like it is, the better it will be for all of you,' Buchanan yelled.

Ivers held up the palm of his hand and with the other he lifted the tray.

'No, not you, her,' Buchanan said, nodding at PC Roberts.

Roberts looked at Ivers who raised his eyebrows as he nodded in the direction of Buchanan. She hesitated. She was aware that it was unusual to offer another potential hostage. She shrugged it off and did as directed. Roberts took the tray and began the short walk to the side room.

Ivers observed and waited. Behind him he adjusted the Tazer that nestled at the base of his back. He was too far away to use it now, and Buchanan was too volatile to consider following Roberts into the room. He'd bide his time and wait. His job was to negotiate not retaliate. At times like these he was controlled and measured. The fact he had a Tazer was only due to his operational deployment as the duty inspector. Buchanan watched closely as PC Roberts entered the side room.

'Hey, Diane, I made sure it was just as you like it, milk and no sugar, right?' Roberts said.

'Shut it with the chat and leave the tray on the floor. Step back out the room.' Buchanan sprayed spittle, as he barked his instructions.

Ivers shifted in readiness to respond should Buchanan make a hostile move. He'd taken a risk he felt was a calculated one. By letting Roberts take the tray, as Buchanan had demanded, he was letting Buchanan believe he was in control, which he wasn't. An armed team were in the next corridor, working through tactics, and in readiness to deploy.

He couldn't control PC Roberts, though, who was now entering the next stage of fatigue.

'You know what? You're one complete and utter arsehole. Have you no shame putting this woman through more than she should ever be going through? Ever questioned why she might be here with police? No, of course you haven't. You just decided your day was shit so why not infect someone else's in the same way.'

Roberts picked up a tea and started to walk towards Diane who was still being held by Buchanan.

'Come any closer, I'll do her. I'll fucking do her.' Buchanan pulled Diane in close and the edge of the blade hovered against her throat.

Roberts stopped and held the tea out towards Diane.

'Just let her have a drink, will you? We can carry on with whatever you want, it's a tea not a bomb for fuck's sake,' Roberts said.

With all the commotion, Buchanan hadn't noticed that Ivers had moved. Buchanan's attention was directed towards PC Roberts, as she stood defiantly and held out the Styrofoam cup while she threw a look of reassurance in the direction of Diane. Her breathing, Roberts noticed, had begun to steady. Buchanan was at a loss. His mind span unsure of what action he should take next. It was still a standoff but Roberts had shifted the dynamic and he didn't like it. Either he let Diane take the tea and risk losing her in a grab by Roberts or he took it himself. Either way he'd have to let her go and Roberts knew this too.

CHAPTER TWENTY-NINE

Nash sat and stared at a mobile phone. It was on top of a mound of paperwork on her desk she really needed to work through but couldn't summon the energy or concentration to do so. It was the very same phone that contained the number that was now causing so much derision and confusion. How did the number that only she knew and had access to, aside from DS Harris, enter the murder enquiries she was investigating?

She got up and turned on a radio that had its home on her window ledge. Someone had changed the station to Classic FM as a joke. They all knew she was a Radio X fan. Barber's *Adagio for Strings* filtered through the speaker. She shook her head as she looked out over the parade ground at a fresh batch of recruits as they prepared for the final pass out parade. The last thing she needed was thoughts of Elias in the throes of death on the killing fields of Vietnam. She turned it off all together. Music wasn't going to help her think today.

She'd sent Moretti away to oversee Matthews's section and ensure all other intelligence leads were being maximised. She sat back down and opened her decision logs. She started to work back through the early entries she'd made. Had she made an error of judgement? Had she missed something obvious with all the plates she'd been spinning? No. She was blessed with a mind that stored and retrieved information easily and enjoyed the retention and gameplay that came with every investigation. The gameplay being to outsmart the killer and shut every door he or she opened.

She grabbed her car keys and jacket. She'd had enough of being indoors and it wasn't helping her mind. As she scanned her desk for her warrant card, there was a cough at her door. The cough belonged to DI Richards from Professional Standards. The message to his department about her DCs hadn't got through, she mused, as he blocked her exit.

'They're not here. I've sent them home. You'll have to wait,' Nash said as she scooped the warrant card's lanyard up from under a plain docket and placed it in her bag.

'You know that should be displayed at all times while in a police building?' Richards retorted.

'The bag or the warrant card? Look, I know you have your job to do but so do I. Their welfare is important as are my investigations and yours. Let's face it, Richards, the two armed robbers survived and will in all likelihood refuse to talk to you,' Nash said.

'You can't wrap your detectives in cotton wool and expect me to ignore the fluff. I will be speaking to them either here or at home, and you had better get used to that,' Richards replied. 'All I've experienced from your team is obstruction. Now I see where they get their direction, it all makes sense. I can be damaging to careers, Detective Inspector. I have the ear of many senior management, very high up the chain.'

He hooked his thumbs over the top of his frayed trouser top. Nash inhaled deeply and Richards smiled as though the message had finally sunk home. How wrong he was.

Nash stepped towards him and stood face-to-face with someone whom she saw as no more than a beachball with a badge that had entered her property for the last time and wouldn't get thrown back inflated.

'I've met many men like you in the job. Men who think they can swan into my domain, as though I'm sat at the wrong desk, and give the same sermon expecting me to drop to my knees and show my appreciation. Well, let me give you a message you can take back to your *chums* in whatever Lodge you've crawled from. Fuck you. I will lead as I always have. From the front. Now shift your arse out of my office. I have murders to investigate. Go and see traffic section and drool over the scene photos from your job. I'll call you as soon as my officers have returned to duty.'

Richards said nothing. His slack jaw unhinged like a python swallowing a rabbit. Nash strode past him. Clarke stood aghast in the main office doorway but held a smile that Nash returned with a wink, as Nash tied back her hair and walked down the corridor to the exit and her car.

* * *

Nash waited in the canteen at NSY for DS Harris to return with her chai latte. She needed a sugar hit after her experience with Richards. There'd been no further contact from him since she'd left the office and a call to the incident room confirmed he'd departed shortly after she'd left. Harris sat opposite her and slid the mug towards her along with a packet of shortbread biscuits.

'I hear you've had a lively time?' he said, as he sipped his latte and wiped the foam on the back of his hand. He ripped open his own packet of biscuits with his teeth and spat the corner out.

Nash stared at him in disgust. 'Carl, have you no grace? News travels quickly for such a large organisation,' she said as she wiped her mouth with a serviette.

'I called George to see if you'd left and he explained everything. Now before you have a go at him for not sticking to the rule of what's said in the office stays in the office, he was proud of the way you stood up for the team. They all heard your speech and felt the same.'

'He had it coming, but to be honest I'm not proud of it. Anyway, it leads me onto our work and a situation you won't be happy with,' she said.

Harris's forehead ridged like a ploughed field and his eyebrows jutted forwards.

'What does that mean?' he said.

'It means, a number I was using for a previous job with you has entered our enquiry,' she said, monitoring his face for the reaction.

Harris was a tough cookie to predict. He rarely let his body language give his thoughts away. Thankfully, today, he'd taken the day off.

'Well, it's not uncommon. Numbers cross over at times on jobs, you know that,' he said.

'Not any old number. My number that I used to communicate with the target on a UC job,' she replied.

She smiled at a DC she'd been through training school with. He didn't come over. He recognised the warmth of the expression wasn't an invitation to join them.

'Oh. That does make it different,' Harris replied, after giving it a little thought.

'The number was a pay-as-you-go SIM. I bought it along with the phone at the shop we're targeting. The number appeared on each of my victims' phone data. The calls are made at the same time on different days and last for the same duration of thirty seconds. I have to account for how it's happened. The number's associated to me and on an intelligence log. One I entered and restricted the access to me alone,' she explained.

Harris sat back and blew out a long sigh as he drew his hands along the top of his coarse tight curls.

'Can't it disappear?' he said as he leaned towards her.

'Carl! I'm serious. This isn't going away, and you'd better get your head around the fact. I'm investigating murder and the number's of significance. Even more so now it's linked to me as the Investigating Officer and was used to call both victims when they were alive! I can't explain it; but the data doesn't lie and neither do I,' she hissed.

Harris studied her.

'I was taking the piss, but I can see it was badly timed. There will be an explanation, you just haven't discovered it yet. How's Matthews and that ticking bomb, Jonesy?'

'They're doing fine – in the circumstances. I sent them home after the hospital debacle. Hopefully they can use the time to reflect and make sure they're fit to be interviewed by DI Richards when the time comes,' she said.

Her phone rang out. She retrieved it from her bag and pressed the green button.

'Nash,' she said.

'DI Nash? This is DCI Jameson from Professional Standards. DS Matthews is suspended from duty until further notice. I've taken the liberty of calling him at home and letting him know. You might want to arrange a welfare visit as he sounded upset.'

Nash cupped the microphone end and turned away from the main canteen and Harris as she replied.

'You lot really are a piece of work, aren't you?' she whispered, with venom.

'Just doing our jobs, Detective Inspector, as are you. The IOPC are also involved. They'll oversee the investigation. Again, I've let DS Matthews know and told him you'll be following up with the paperwork for his suspension. I've completed it and sent it through to you by email to print and have him sign at your next welfare visit. Have a good day, ma'am, and we'll be in touch after we've spoken to both officers,' he said.

Nash turned back and rested her neck over the back of the low faux leather seat.

'Do what you have to. But let me tell you this, if any of your goons go over the top with either of them, then I will be paying you a visit rather than hiding behind a phone, and it won't be pretty. Good day,' she said, terminating the call.

'Trouble at mill?' Harris asked.

'The flour's off along with the top baker,' she replied as she grabbed her bag and got up.

Harris gently put a hand on her arm as she started to leave.

'You're better than them, Pip, don't lose your head with their mind games. Remember our training. You were top of the class and we pushed you far harder than anyone else on the undercover course.'

'I should make you iron this blouse.' She smiled, then leaned over and kissed the top of his head as she left.

Harris wiped his forehead, then ran his hand along his trousers as he looked around the room with an air of embarrassment.

CHAPTER THIRTY

'Why don't you place the cups on the floor, PC Roberts, and step out of the room.' The voice of Ivers interrupted the stale air. He was carrying two plates that contained a sandwich on each that he set down on a desk.

PC Roberts did as directed. Buchanan didn't move. Ivers had hoped he would so they could grab him while he was away from Diane. It wasn't to be.

Ivers sat in a chair, leaned back and pushed one of the plates towards Roberts.

Buchanan's eyes stuck out from his skull at the sight and smell of grilled bacon. Diane took no notice. Buchanan shifted his concentration to Ivers.

'I suppose you think you're gonna smoke me out by eating one of your own eh, pig?' Buchanan's head rocked back in laughter as he chuckled at his own joke. A strand of saliva escaped the side of his mouth. His dry tongue licked it away.

Ivers was confident he'd taste victory. A taste above and beyond anything a hospital bacon roll provided. He also had a team in the background frantically working to bring a resolution to the situation. That team wouldn't be engaged in talk though. If they were deployed, then Ivers had failed.

'You better have called that cab, copper, cause if you ain't then that'll be the last bit of grub you'll be scarfing,' Buchanan said.

'Mr Buchanan, the best advice I can give you is to stop. The police have the resources to carry on all night and day for as long as it takes, but do you? Stop now. We can talk outside of these surroundings and let the hospital get back to treating the sick, like Diane, who really does need medical help. Why don't you let her go?' Ivers said, his hands held out in a gesture of goodwill that let the bacon scent drift.

'Ha! What you mean is throw in the towel and you'll drag me out of here and back to the cells in handcuffs. Well, fuck you, cause that ain't gonna happen,' Buchanan said.

Ivers ignored him. He could see Diane was fading.

'Diane could really do with seeing a doctor. Your argument isn't with her, it's with us, the police,' Ivers said.

Buchanan said nothing so Ivers continued.

'I'm going to send PC Roberts for a break.' Ivers nodded at Roberts.

She hesitated, then slid off the desk and walked towards the main doors to the ward where armed officers gathered either side and formed a corridor for her to walk through. The lead armed officers who'd opened the swing doors pushed rubber door wedges in place. The doors remained open and all chatter subsided to nought.

CHAPTER THIRTY-ONE

Moretti checked his watch. Nash had been gone a while and he guessed whom she was meeting. Clarke had returned to her desk and sported a fixed grimace of a smile ever since she'd overheard Nash and Richards going head-to-head. Moretti turned back to the paperwork on the desk and the charts Clarke had created.

Somehow he'd try and make sense of how Nash's covert number had appeared on Melissa and Jade's call data. They were getting nowhere with the investigation. Buchanan was still the main attraction of his travelling circus, where he was doing a great job of being a clown. Moretti was starting to think that Nash was more concerned with her UC role and DS than being the Investigating Officer for murder. Maybe she was looking to leave the team and join Harris fulltime, as the undercover unit were down a DI. He rubbed the top of his head and walked to the coffee machine. A new batch was in preparation and the sweet smell of fresh percolated coffee beans had become too much to resist.

'Do you want a top-up, George?' Moretti asked as he held a mug up to the light and risk-assessed whether he needed to wash it or not. He decided he'd take the risk and waited for the black nectar to fill the jug.

'I'm good thanks, Nick, but I appreciate the offer. How's the Instagram enquiry coming along?' Sagona asked. He stopped typing and let his glasses on a cord drop around his neck.

'Slowly. I know where Matthews was coming from, but I don't get how this links with our killer. There's certainly nothing to connect Buchanan with the victims' accounts. I just can't see a man like him going to those lengths,' Moretti explained.

'I know what you mean. I've been going through what we have on HOLMES and that isn't helping much. Sometimes I can see a pattern of evidence or associations building up, but this time it's very disconnected, apart from the MO for both Jade and Melissa. I get what you're saying with Buchanan, like, I know his boots showed trace evidence from Melissa's flat, but he's given a prepared statement. That alone would be strong in court even when challenged by a decent prosecution barrister.' Sagona scooted his chair closer to where Moretti was sitting and ducked low as he spoke.

'It's this other number that's marked as protected… How on earth can that be?' Sagona sat up again. His spine cracked as he leaned back and stretched his stumpy legs.

Moretti knew Sagona had a point. He wasn't the first of the team to seek Moretti's counsel on the subject. Moretti intended to find out. When he'd established the facts, he'd make certain it was all disclosed properly to the prosecution barrister if Buchanan was charged with murder.

He also gave consideration to Buchanan not being the killer. Moretti had been back to the exhibits store on one of his whims and retrieved all the personal property that related to Buchanan. In particular, he was interested in his phone. What Moretti confirmed was that the phone Buchanan had in his possession wasn't a smartphone but a cheap throwaway one.

The other searches they'd completed hadn't revealed a computer either. Buchanan had a website and a Facebook page as they'd already established. Matthews had undertaken further research on the website's originator. He had established it was from a free start-up offer a website company had designed, keen to assist ex-offenders in the creation of any new business venture, as long as it was legal. There were no subscription fees for Buchanan to be concerned with as the company took care of that. It was a home page only, with a description of his services and a contact number.

Moretti was back at his own desk. He tried calling Nash but there was no reply. He heard noises coming from the corridor. He got up and walked towards the incident room door and the corridor where DS Matthews's voice reverberated off the walls.

'Where's Nash?' Matthews shouted loudly as he burst through the incident room door.

Moretti grabbed his arm and moved him towards a storeroom. Matthews offered weak resistance to Moretti's strength. Moretti opened the door and ushered Matthews in, kicking the door closed behind him.

'What in the fuck are you doing coming back here yawping the house down?' Moretti demanded, standing nose-to-nose with him.

'I want to see Nash. I want to know why she agreed on my suspension from duty without any kind of a fight on my behalf,' he said as he looked over Moretti's shoulder at the closed door, figuring a way past to Nash's office.

Moretti pointed at a seat behind Matthews. A seat Moretti had put there for times when he needed space to gather his thoughts.

'Take a seat and calm down, will you,' Moretti said.

Matthews shook his head and reluctantly sat. Moretti could see the red flush leave Matthews's cheeks. Moretti crouched so he wasn't towering over him. He liked Matthews and could see his performance was out of character. A reaction born out of stress rather than any real animosity towards Nash.

'Pip would've had no say in the decision, and for what it's worth, she gave DI Richards an absolute mouthful when he arrived here demanding to know why she'd sent you two home. She told him not to make contact with you until she'd had a chance to see you both. For all I know, she could be on her way to you now as her phone's not being answered and I've no idea where she is,' Moretti said.

Matthews's head hung over the low-backed chair as he rested his neck and stared at the ceiling.

'What the fuck's going on, Nick? I did what anyone else would've done in the circumstances. Any other copper would've got away with it, but not me, oh no, not me – I get the book smashed over my skull until I'm pleading submission,' he said.

He ran his hands over his hair and tugged at his widow's peak as he sat back into the rough fabric of the chair and exhaled. Moretti let him have some time to compose himself. At some point, they'd have to leave the isolation booth Moretti had created and return to the outside world.

'Look, I'll speak to Pip and let her know how you're feeling. Being here isn't going to do you any favours and if Richards is on the prowl, he'll take the opportunity to ambush you and you don't need that. Just go home and sit tight while you figure out the account you'll give to Richards's team. I know a very good Fed Rep. He'll help you every step of the way. I can call him once you've gone and get him to contact you. What do you say?'

Matthews looked up at Moretti. Moretti could see Matthews was struggling to compose himself. Moretti reached and tapped the side of his arm below the shoulder by way of reassurance and got up.

'Shut the door after you and for fuck's sake don't let on about this space as everyone will want to be in here,' Moretti joked as he left Matthews to take five before he left the building.

Moretti moved further down the corridor away from the incident room and took out his mobile. He dialled the Fed Rep as he'd promised. As the man he wanted answered, Matthews walked past and disappeared down the stairs to the block and out onto the parade square.

CHAPTER THIRTY-TWO

The armed officer pointed two fingers at his eyes and then at the corridor beyond the open doors to the ward. His colleague opposite nodded at the signal as he shifted his feet and stretched his neck from side to side in readiness for the assault. Buchanan's voice was all that could be heard echoing along the empty ward as he bellowed at Ivers to bring PC Roberts back. Ivers sat and gave a good show of convincing Buchanan that he was listening but all the time he was concentrating on Diane, assessing how she was coping. He wondered whether the decision to continue the negotiation was about to be removed from his jurisdiction and transferred to the firearms team who were congregated like an armed conga troupe within his peripheral vision.

Ivers didn't want to be anywhere near Buchanan when they stormed the ward. Ivers knew they'd managed to feed a fibre optic camera into the room Buchanan and Diane were in. All he could do was try and keep both Diane and Buchanan alive. That was his primary objective and as he sat distracted by the armed officers, he wondered whether he was going to succeed or not.

As Diane sat on the hospital bed, her eyes began to flicker as though she'd snapped out of a haze. Her brain had been working overtime in an effort to interpret a smell. A smell that had bothered her the moment Buchanan had entered the ward.

Roberts had asked her if there was anything distinctive about her assailant, anything that she could remember that would assist them to identify him. The attack had been brutal. So much so that she'd closed her eyes and tried to stay conscious. At the times she'd opened them she couldn't see him, but only sensed his breath. Her mind was back in the present. Suddenly, she felt as though she was in the middle of a stadium when the floodlights were activated. Her assailant had a distinctive smell. Engine oil. She'd thought she was getting flashbacks to the attack but it was here in the room and had been ever since Buchanan had taken hold of her. This wasn't the first time they'd met without an introduction. She looked at Buchanan who'd forgotten she was there as he paced the room in front of the door and gesticulated at Ivers as he shouted his demands, and waved the scalpel in front of him emphasising each word.

Diane let her concentration settle within the room. It was clinically clean, with very little to use against her captor. Then she curled her fingers on the bedding and she smiled.

Ivers had noticed the shift in Diane's behaviour and he made sure Buchanan remained focussed on him.

'I'm doing all that can be done at this time. I'm as frustrated as you are that it isn't happening as quickly as we'd both hoped it would. You have to understand that to get any taxi driver to agree to come to this hospital to collect a man armed with a blade isn't the easiest of asks,' Ivers said, by way of explanation.

As Ivers continued, Diane slowly inched towards the rear of the bed and a chart that was attached along with a biro.

CHAPTER THIRTY-THREE

Nash dropped her forensic face shield and leaned against the concrete balcony wall. She placed her elbows on the top and stretched her shoulders as she breathed in some air. The balcony ran along the width of the block that housed two hundred occupants on a South London estate. It provided access and egress for the residents of the fourth floor. It was an estate that functioned the way most did in London. Today wasn't a day anyone had imagined would play out the way it had.

Detectives in forensic suits swarmed all over the flat after the alarm had been raised by a relative who'd arrived with their own key. They'd been contacted by a charity where the occupant, their daughter, worked. The charity hadn't heard from the occupant for a couple of days. She'd not been at work or called in sick, which was unusual for someone who was rarely off. Bryony Moore was a much-loved youth worker who'd provided a key service for the estate's young people but had now been given an enforced retirement at the hands of a killer. Her mother had found her only daughter in the bathroom. Her daughter's hair bobbed on the surface, as loose strands of Titian curls clawed at the sides of the bath as though they were looking for an escape from the watery grave.

She'd been killed by way of strangulation. The same MO as Melissa Phelps and Jade Williams. The estate was within walking distance of their blocks. The balcony was sealed off with crime scene tape, and a uniformed officer stood calmly as he held a clipboard that supported a crime scene log. Residents keen to understand why police were there, strained necks like giant tortoises in an effort to get a better view. Some held phones on sticks. The officer ignored those that did. His job was to secure the scene, not to police the right to film, despite his aversion to the activity.

The deceased was carried out on a covered stretcher. A baby could be heard crying from an adjacent flat as a blackbird accompanied it in song from a communal washing line far below. The officer on the cordon turned away from the crowd as he heard people say there was something happening behind him. As the body of Bryony Moore was taken over the threshold of her flat for the final time, he removed his hat and held it up obscuring the phone on a stick. There was a limit to what he would accept as a right of free will.

Nash remained on the balcony as the stretcher's casters bumped over the threshold to the door. She dropped her facemask and let her gloved hands rest in front of her stomach as she lowered her eyes. When she raised them again, she saw JJ was following behind the stretcher carrying a cat basket. It was a sight that Nash felt was all too familiar. Once they'd left, she replaced her overshoes with a fresh set, pulled up her mask and re-entered the flat. Inside, Moretti was engaged in conversation with Yvonne Campbell, the SOCO, as they discussed the instructions Nash had given them for her forensic priorities prior to stepping outside.

Moretti noticed she'd returned, and left Campbell to her work as he joined Nash. They were in the small living room. Nash nodded at the detective to hand her the exhibits book. Nash flicked through the pages, using each individual entry as her guide as to what had been collated so far. It consisted of correspondence, but also a laptop computer and a mobile phone, along with some billing history in the form of paper bills. A diary had also been found. Nash handed the log back to the detective and turned to Moretti.

'I've spoken to Sally and given her the details of the victim's Instagram account and password; it had been written down in a separate book along with one for her computer. Of course, you know what this means?' Nash said.

Moretti nodded. 'Buchanan isn't our man. For this job anyway,' he said.

Nash showed her agreement with a bob of her head.

'I've had the control room that covers the hospital where Buchanan is, on the phone. He's still there holding court and making demands. He's getting nowhere with the cab, and an armed entry team is getting restless, so it could be over very soon, which leaves me with some decisions to make,' Nash said.

Her phone started to vibrate and she answered it. It was DS Harris, who sounded like he'd finished a tough set of squats. Nash stepped out of the room and went into the kitchen to take the call.

'Pip?' Harris asked.

'It's me, what's up?'

'I've had a breakthrough and need to see you,' Harris said as he regained his breath.

Nash could hear the sounds of traffic in the background and realised he must have been running. Nash cupped her hand near her chin and curved her palm around her mouth as she spoke.

'I'm in the middle of *another* murder scene. I can't, and *won't*, drop it for anything you've got going on that involves bent phones,' she hissed through the voice piece.

No one looking would've seen her eyes bulge at the top of her mask as she spoke. The nerve of the man was unreal, she thought.

'Oi, keep your mask on. This is in relation to your jobs and could help your dynamic duo Matthews and his side prick, Jonesy. I don't want to talk on the phone,' Harris said.

Nash took a deep breath as she evaluated where she was in terms of this crime scene. The rest of the team had swung into action rapidly and all immediate enquiries were being undertaken. She could leave the main scene with Moretti who'd taken the initial call and managed it very well prior to her arrival.

'Are you at the Italian?' she asked.

'Where else would I be when we need a meet?'

'I'll see you there. This better be good or I won't hold back my anger regardless of where we are.'

CHAPTER THIRTY-FOUR

When Nash arrived at the cafe, Harris was already on his second latte and a slab of shortbread. He'd done the decent thing and bought her a slice of the cheesecake that she loved. When he saw her approach the door from his prime seat, he turned to the owner and ordered her a chai latte. Nash strode through the door and weaved through the tables to where Harris was sitting. He was all smiles and charm as she approached and sat down.

'I hope you washed your hands,' Harris said with a wry smirk as she settled in and pulled the cheesecake towards her.

Nash lifted the small cake fork and aimed it at Harris like Neptune's trident.

'Shut it, you. I've no mood for your smarm or sarcasm. I'm having a bitch of a time. I am in the mood for this cheesecake and a fresh chai latte, though,' she said as the drink landed before her.

Nash thanked the waiter and looked at Harris over the rim of the cup as she took a sip.

'You've surprised me, thank you,' she said.

Nash felt guilty as she sat and enjoyed the normality of life while her team grafted and the Moore family grieved. She snapped out of it quickly as she knew this was work and not a social visit and she had to eat. The mind could be a bastard at times, she surmised.

'Let's get down to business, shall we? I don't have long and please knock that childish grin off your face. You know exactly what I mean,' Nash said.

She took out a plain pad from her bag rather than her daybook. It was fitting for the setting and one she'd used since the inception of the covert operation. It kept her jobs apart and she wouldn't risk picking up the wrong book for the wrong investigation.

'So, what is it you've established?' she asked.

Harris looked about the cafe before he replied. It was quiet for the time of day. A few stragglers sat away from them and were engrossed in their phones.

Harris leaned down and picked up his own man-bag. He took out a non-descript, red hardback book. He pushed it towards Nash and Nash opened it. Inside were a series of images taken from a covert camera. The lead images were of the front of the phone shop they'd been targeting. She noticed that the dates generated by the camera's processor were from a month ago; the time and date digitally stamped in the bottom right corner of each still image. She continued to turn the pages while Harris left her to it, looking out the window misted from condensation.

She turned another page. Staring up at her was the face of Melissa Phelps. She wore dark shades, a casual coat and skinny fit jeans. She was pictured exiting the phone shop. Nash looked up at Harris who nodded at her to keep turning. She did so, and on the next page was Jade Williams. She was dressed in a dark suit and overcoat.

None of the women appeared as though they were being subversive, just exiting a shop that sold mobile phones. Nash turned another page, which was blank. She sat back and pushed the book away, as though it contained porn she didn't wish to view. This feeling didn't last long as her curiosity overwhelmed her and she dragged the book back and opened it again just to satisfy her questioning mind that what she'd seen was accurate. Harris observed how Nash had taken in the images and how perplexed she looked.

'I thought about our last conversation and how you wanted the outstanding from the robbery identified and nicked,' he said. 'I tasked the Ops team to review all the covert camera footage from the observation point that covered the phone shop, primarily looking for any smash and grabbers that frequented the place. They agreed, naturally, and this was an unexpected revelation. I couldn't believe it myself when I saw the images. To be fair, it was nothing to do with my detective ability. All down to a keen-eyed DC on the operational team. He'd seen the witness appeals your people had created on the police Intranet. I'd never have twigged that they were your victims but this DC's got a reputation for CCTV work, hence he was tasked on that role. He then decided to look at Jade Williams's photo and compare it to the only Jamaican female he'd seen in her age bracket enter the shop, and he couldn't understand what he'd come up with.' Harris paused and took a sip of coffee as he let Nash digest the information.

'So, both of my victims used the shop before they were murdered,' Nash said. She looked out of the window while she pondered how this would fit with her investigation. The shop was a phone shop. It wasn't beyond possibility that they'd heard about the place and decided to use it. The prices were good and times hard. One of them maybe, but both of them seemed a stretch. The professions they were in would also appear to be out of character for the clientele the shop attracted. Both women could easily afford a new phone and upgrade whenever they wished. They were on a professional London wage.

'What's your take on it?' Nash asked.

Harris sat back and placed his palms behind his head. He interlocked his fingers as he thought about the question she'd posed. He dropped back closer to her before he spoke.

'In all honesty I don't know yet, but I don't believe in coincidence. There's something about this shop and those it attracts that makes me uncomfortable,' Harris said, which wasn't of any help to Nash other than to confirm the signals her gut was firing were accurate.

'What do we know about the shop? Who owns it? Is it leased? By whom, when, for how long, how's it paid for, who else works there in addition to the two we've met?' she asked rapidly, as her brain generated each question.

'I'll need to know if the latest victim frequented the place. I'll get a photo to you to give to the DC on the operational team who's doing this CCTV work. How are we going to manage this now, Carl? This investigation has crossed over to murder. I have an idea how I'd like it managed but I'm willing to work with you while I can,' she said.

Harris appreciated the position she was in. He'd supplied covert camera footage that was now considered of relevance to her murder enquiries. It wasn't a major issue at the present time, but could be if charges were brought and the shop had a greater meaning in the investigations. Something neither knew right now, but it needed to be aired as a potential issue.

'Look, murder trumps robbery, so however you want to play it, you have my support,' Harris said, and Nash could tell by his face that it was genuinely meant and not an attempt to fob her off then carry on alone and ignore her investigations.

'I'll get Moretti involved,' Nash said. 'I can't manage everything and that way he can see that I'm not trying to hide anything either, as there's still the issue of my covert number entering the murder investigations, and that issue hasn't been resolved. I'll need to meet with the CPS and get some early advice. I know a good band E lawyer, they'll grasp the issues quickly and advise appropriately,' she said.

Nash sent Moretti a text and he responded that he could meet in the next two hours back at the office. She replied that she'd see him there. Harris paid and they left the cafe. Nash headed to the underground at Vauxhall and as she descended the steps down to the escalator to the tube platform, she wondered where all this new information was headed. She had the book Harris had brought with him in her bag. She gripped it between her underarm and the side of her chest as she flashed her warrant card at the gate attendant who let her through. She stepped onto the escalator that conveyed her down to the train's platform.

CHAPTER THIRTY-FIVE

The armed entry team were still in the corridor. There came the sound of a crash of doors in the distance. Buchanan stopped talking; his senses alert to the change from noise of his own making to that of something new.

'What was that?' he demanded.

Ivers turned towards the noise.

'I've been listening to you so haven't a clue. It is a hospital, though, so probably another admission that is being turned away because you're still insistent on locking down an entire ward,' Ivers said as he turned back to Buchanan.

Ivers noticed a faint smile had appeared on Diane's face. She'd slowly shuffled back away from the end of the bed as Buchanan stared back at him with a puzzled look.

'I'm not here for fun!' Buchanan said.

'Well, that's the first thing we can agree on,' Ivers muttered as he heard the familiar sound of a heeled shoe on the hospital's linoleum floor.

Nash approached the armed officer who was stationed beyond the main doors to the ward. The sentry had been informed by personal radio that Nash was coming through. He'd radioed for another armed officer to join him and escort Nash to the temporary operational command room that had been set up in the nurses' staff room.

'So? Who is it?' Buchanan demanded.

He wouldn't venture beyond the self-imposed boundary line he'd created in his mind while in the room.

'Your guess is as good as mine,' Ivers replied.

'Well, it better be the taxi driver is all I'll say,' Buchanan said as he sat back down next to Diane and wiped the handle of the scalpel blade on his trousers.

* * *

Nash greeted the main commander for the operation: a young-looking superintendent. They sat down at the table. It was adorned with an architectural map of the ward and a portable TV screen that showed a top-down view of the room Buchanan and Diane were in. The image was being routed back courtesy of a fibre optic cable that had been covertly installed behind the scenes while Buchanan was having a rant.

The superintendent noticed Nash observing the screen.

'Just in case this runs for days and we actually storm it,' he said, as though he needed to justify his actions to another officer of rank that attended.

'Well, I have some news that may help bring this to an end,' Nash said as she accepted a mug of tea placed in front of her.

The superintendent waved a hand politely to intimate that he was good as far as refreshment was concerned.

'I hope you've arrived with a resolution, Detective Inspector, as I'm fast running out of options,' he said.

'I've had another murder. Similar MO to the other two and it can't have been Buchanan. He was here under police guard. The pathologist has provided an approximate time of death and now that's officially recorded, I'm here to ensure Buchanan gets the message and see if we can't end this standoff. I've called his solicitor. She's not going to attend as she's with another client,' Nash said.

'Well, thank God for that. Just the kind of news I need to put this to bed,' he said, beginning to clear the table of papers.

'What are you doing?' Nash asked.

'I'm wrapping this up sharpish and giving the hospital back its ward,' he replied.

'I wouldn't be so hasty if I were you,' Nash suggested.

He sat back down with a frown.

'Well, surely he can be bailed from here?' he asked, in a vain hope she'd say yes.

'He's wanted for charging in relation to a rape, and a recent search of a garage, to which he had access, would tend to suggest he hasn't stopped. Obviously he's assaulted Diane while he's held her against her will, so I would also suggest further charges are appropriate,' Nash said.

'Of course… of course. How will you tell him?' he said.

'Me?' Nash replied.

'Yes, you. Who else is going to break the news to him?' he asked, perplexed that she should suggest a man of his rank deal directly with a member of the public.

Nash leaned towards him and composed herself before she replied.

'If I waltz in there like one of the girls at the boxing who gets to announce the next round, he's likely to hit the roof. According to him, I've destroyed his life. I'm no longer on his Christmas card list. No matter what way you look at it, to him, it's nothing but a shit sandwich and I'm no waitress,' Nash replied.

She'd learned very early on in her career that if she sat back and took on board every request a senior officer made to duck work, she'd never get anywhere. She wasn't about to be left holding this baby. She could see by his wide eyes he wasn't going to accept her statement, so she hammered her position home.

'I'm the Investigating Officer for three murders. I have a team awaiting my direction. This is not a message *I* need to deliver. I'm only here so you can hear the update from me in person rather than by phone. Messages have a habit of getting lost in translation. I have no way to prove Buchanan did the other two murders. His prepared statement is convincing and corroborates the forensic evidence for one of my murder scenes. I'm not interested in charging the wrong person. Other information has surfaced that my team will now react to that may negate his involvement. That man is wasting valuable police time. I think it's about time his rave was shut down, don't you?' she said as she got up and gathered her bag and coat.

The superintendent looked flustered, and behind Nash the firearms team leader stifled a laugh with a cough as he left the room to save face.

The superintendent found his voice. 'I will speak with Inspector Ivers, get his take on who'd be best to relay the information to Buchanan. I appreciate it won't be you, DI Nash. Thank you for coming out of your way to update me. Try a phone next time. Now, if you'll excuse me, I have work to do,' he said, taking his flat hat from the chair where it sat and placing it on his head.

All braid and bluster, Nash thought as he strode past her towards the ward that Ivers was in. The superintendent's bag carrier closely followed behind him juggling bits of paper. Nash smiled at the only other officer left in the room who'd raised her head.

'Do tell the superintendent it was a marvellous cup of tea, and that I've let the borough Sapphire team DI know that Buchanan's theirs now. If I need him, he's going nowhere fast, so nothing's lost,' she said before walking out of the staff room, leaving the door open.

As Nash left the room she heard an almighty scream coming from the ward where Buchanan was. It was the voice of a female. A female who was in pain. Nash deduced it could only have come from Diane.

Nash ran towards the sound and as she rounded the wall of the corridor towards the ward, she saw a firearms officer. Nash slowed up and put her hands out at chest height, palms out, to indicate she understood the request and wouldn't move beyond the imposed line he'd resurrected by the barrel of his MP5 submachine gun. He hadn't raised it fully, but halfway was enough for her. She could hear voices. Buchanan was dragged out.

His wrists were thrust back-to-back behind him in plasti-cuffs. Blood streamed from his left eye which was a bloodshot mess. Buchanan was being supported under the armpits by two firearms officers, his feet sliding along the floor as he refused to walk. Ivers followed out behind them. Ivers held Diane by the shoulders as he talked calmly to her. Diane looked visibly shaken and her face and top was marked with blood.

'Diane, it's DI Nash, where have you been hurt?'

Ivers lowered Diane onto a seat that was placed near her by a nurse. Diane wasn't physically injured. The blood was all Buchanan's, from where Diane had plunged a Bic biro into his eye socket. She'd used the distraction of the superintendent's stammered speech to launch her attack. She would have gouged Buchanan's eye out had Ivers not dragged her off him. Diane looked up to see PC Roberts. Roberts had been asleep in a restroom as she was too tired to go home, and the nurse who'd tended to her insisted she used it.

PC Roberts moved forwards and held her hands.

'It's all going to be good, Diane. He can't harm you anymore,' she said as Diane looked into her eyes and finally let her courage and strength dissolve, and her tears fall.

CHAPTER THIRTY-SIX

Moretti waited in the hospital car park for Nash to appear. As she did, he flashed the lights of the non-descript car he was in. Nash walked over, pleased to see him. He'd texted to say he'd collect her. Nash ducked into the warmth of the car. In the central cup holder was a takeaway coffee.

Nash savoured the scent before she took a sip and looked across at Moretti. 'Thanks, Nick, you're a saviour. I needed a lift and the drink's a bonus after the dry atmosphere in that hospital. Thankfully, Diane's no longer at risk of harm from that idiot,' she said.

Moretti engaged reverse and backed out of the bay.

'I heard the superintendent in charge was as effective as the current government in a crisis,' he said as he indicated right and exited the hospital to join the traffic into Central London.

Nash looked in the side mirror and let out a sigh of relief as the entrance to the hospital dissolved to a distant memory.

'Any other news?' she asked.

Moretti wriggled his back into a comfortable position for the journey to the office.

'I had a call from a DC on the operational team involved in the phone shop job,' he said, switching lane to avoid a cyclist. 'I'd sent him a photo of the last victim. She's also caught on camera entering and exiting the shop. It's definitely linked. Why, is still unknown.'

'What about her social media? Is that the same as the others?' Nash asked.

'She has an Instagram account and it's private like the other two. She also has a cat, as you know, and she has posted pictures in the same way–'

'But?' Nash interjected.

'But… I looked at just how easy it is to see where and when these images were taken, and it isn't quite as straightforward as I first thought. Well, not to me, anyway. I think it goes deeper than a simple image search on Google and the data appearing. Especially when the accounts are locked down in the way theirs were. There's another issue that's greater than that.'

'Well, I'm here and going nowhere fast, so you may as well deliver the bad news,' Nash said.

'Your number is on Moore's call data,' Moretti added.

'The same number that appears on Melissa's and Jade's?'

'Yep.'

Nash shook her head then turned to Moretti.

'I know what you're thinking, Nick. I'd be thinking the same if the tables were turned. I haven't used that number since the operation it was assigned to. I don't know any of the victims outside of work. The first time I ever met them, they were dead. Before you ask, no, I wasn't the last person to see them alive,' she said, as she relaxed her head against the headrest and reached for her coffee.

Moretti noticed and assisted her by handing her the cup.

'I believe you, Pip. We need to prove it though. I've requested your call data for the number from the phone you used on that operation. It hasn't come through as yet, but that should show that no calls were made to any of our victims' numbers, unless you used a different phone with that SIM card in,' Moretti added.

Nash didn't reply. She was glad he'd used his initiative and made the request.

'Who authorised it?' she asked, out of curiosity.

'DCI Carlson. He'll sign anything when he's in a rush for the golf course,' Moretti said with a glint in his eye and a smirk that told Nash she should check what she signed more thoroughly whenever Moretti presented her with a docket to sign off when she was in a hurry.

It was right what they said about the quiet ones being the ones to watch, she thought.

'It's a sad day when the SIO isn't interested in enquiries he's got overall responsibility for,' she said.

'He knows you do a great job and have never let him or the command down,' Moretti added.

'He won't support my promotion though. He's made that quite clear.'

'Why would he? If he did that he'd be out of a job, and no longer free to book out on enquiries that start at the clubhouse and end at the same place,' Moretti said.

The traffic had now opened up and Moretti looked across at Nash and down at a set of switches situated on the dashboard.

'Go on, have your fun,' she remarked, as she settled back into the seat.

Moretti flicked a couple of switches. A hue of blue light sparked from their vehicle, as a repetition of aggressive octaves screamed from the external speakers and announced Moretti's call to arms.

* * *

The team had assembled in the briefing room. Nash had made efficient use of her travel time as she'd been rocked about by Moretti's drive back to the office. She'd made calls to various departments involved in her investigations. She obtained the updates she required before she'd make a decision on her next course of action. A course she hoped would lead to the arrest and charge of their murderer. She'd spoken to Clarke, who'd updated Nash on the developments she'd unearthed through her research. Nash tasked Sagona with calling the team in for a briefing.

She wanted every member of her team brought up to speed. With Buchanan in custody, but effectively written out of her investigation strategy, she needed to focus her attention on the phone shop.

The air in the briefing room fizzed with mixed voices that subsided to a low whisper as Nash and Moretti entered. Nash took her usual seat at the head of the conference table and waited for the projector screen at the opposite end of the meeting room to lower while her team got comfortable. She could tell by the change of energy in the room that they expected to be making progress after this meeting. Much had stalled since Buchanan had been in hospital and the forensic and witness appeals had dried up to nothing. The last scene had been quick to complete, such was the similarity in setting they'd all experienced at the others. That wasn't to say they were apathetic in their approach – far from it. They were as judicious as they'd always been.

Nash nodded at Moretti. He'd activated his laptop that was linked to the main screen. He'd asked Clarke to collate all the research the Intelligence Desk had compiled. She'd done this and uploaded it to his laptop. Both Nash and Moretti hoped Clarke's work would convince them all that they'd take a different path. A path that would be clean and untainted by Buchanan. As Moretti waited for his computer to link with the main projector screen, Clarke entered the room. She took off her headphones and leaned in towards Nash's ear. She spoke in a hushed tone to Nash, who then smiled and nodded at her. Clarke took a deep breath and walked up to the front of the table. The team ignored her and focussed their concentration on the screen that now displayed a PowerPoint presentation she had compiled. Nash announced the meeting was to begin.

'The last scene was identical in many ways to the other two. The same MO as Melissa and Jade. Death by asphyxiation caused by strangulation. Dr King is satisfied to link all three cases,' Nash said, as she looked around the room.

There was no disagreement from anyone and she was surprised that Sagona remained silent. She grasped the lull and continued.

'Buchanan is in custody and being dealt with by the borough Sapphire team. He awaits interview in relation to the rape of Diane Fullerton whom he'd held hostage at St Thomas's Hospital. Early forensic examination of the scene and clothing taken from Diane worn at the time of the rape, showed signs of trace contact. Whether that's fibres or DNA, I don't know, but he's going nowhere. As for our investigation, I've spoken with the CPS and they've suggested we consider bail. However, I'm letting our warrant of further detention continue until I'm satisfied he's not our man, and I have something in writing from the band E lawyer. Although we have the forensic evidence from Melissa's flat on his boots, it isn't enough. He gave a prepared statement that correlated with the evidence we found. Now, before you all start firing back that he would have done as he knew what we'd found, it's not that simple. He's a nasty piece of work but it doesn't make him a killer. He'd carried out bathroom work at both Melissa's and Jade's flats. Correspondence found in Jade's flat and an image of said correspondence sent to me electronically, while coming here, corroborates this. An entry in a diary also showed that he was paid. She'd noted how glad she was to be rid of him. She recorded feeling uncomfortable when he was around, but needed her bathroom work done. He was cheap and turned up where others had let her down. Phone data and a follow-up call also revealed she'd spoken to a client after this diary entry, and she'd met with this client. In other words, Buchanan wasn't the last person to see her alive, nor was he the client she'd met.' Nash paused and let the team make a note of what she'd relayed.

Moretti scribed for her. She wanted him to note down what she said, as she needed to be certain she'd covered everything. He could nudge her if she'd missed a point. She was confident she'd cover everything as she felt her mind was like a new razor. She had an idea where and who they'd focus on.

'I'm going to hand you over to Sally. She's requested a desire to impart the work she's done on the team's behalf, and mine as the IO. Sally, the floor is yours. Take your time,' Nash said.

Clarke had positioned herself so she wouldn't have to look at the main room, but just the screen. Her hands moved as though she'd be better off wearing gloves, despite the ambient temperature of the room. She massaged the computer's infrared pointer in her fingers, then she clicked at the screen and the first slide began.

The team watched as the research was presented. Clarke thought that too much attention was being paid to the cats each victim had owned, as well as the times the images were taken and subsequently uploaded. Many people owned pets and posted pictures of them on social media, so why should this be any different? It all appeared to be more of a coincidence once she'd delved deeper into the background for each victim. That research hadn't highlighted any significant areas of concern in relation to lifestyle, but there was one aspect in relation to Melissa Phelps that was niggling at Clarke. She'd left it out of the presentation but would update Nash afterwards.

The links and data patterns that had originally proposed the killer was accessing their profiles, now seemed implausible. The victims' behaviour was more that of habit, and de-stressing after work. Each image showed their friends that they were at home, back with the pet they cared for. Clarke didn't have any pets, but she could relate to the sense of calm and enjoyment she'd feel when she arrived at her flat, and logged into the online gaming world she adored. Her virtual friends helped her unwind. She didn't post about it on social media though.

She turned back to Nash for the first time since she'd begun. Nash nodded that she was good to finish with her presentation. Nash stood and leaned on the table, all eyes were now back with her.

'I know that there's been debate as to how I have come into this enquiry. I want to reassure you all I haven't, but a number I have used has,' Nash said. 'I can now disclose why, but not yet how. I have been part of a covert investigation that has crossed over to ours. What is about to be disclosed will not leave this room. I'm passing around a memorandum of understanding I expect everyone to read and sign before I continue. If there are any dissenters, then you may leave now.'

Nash waited while the sheets were passed around. Eyes scanned the document and everyone signed and passed them back. Nash continued.

'The address shown on the sheet you've signed, and the operational name, pertains to a phone shop in the city taking in stolen phones for export abroad. Phones obtained by lorry jacking and street robbery. We are talking millions of pounds' worth of goods, not to mention the trauma to every victim robbed on the street or in a shop. This shop in particular is associated with each of our victims.'

Nash looked at the faces of her team, all of which were attentive and alert.

'I tasked Sally by phone to initiate enquiries with Interpol. In particular, any background on the father and son team who operated the phone shop. This work has been completed. The owner is called Kamal Ramiz. An image is on screen now. He's fifty-five, divorced, and known to the Albanian authorities. He's been a person of interest for drug supply and the sale of firearms. He's never been arrested in Albania, but Interpol hold intelligence reports of his associates, many of whom would use the small electrical shop that he ran there to launder money. Outside of work, his passion was cats. Kamal was a breeder of Abyssinian cats and took great pride in attending any show he could to display his breeding line. He travelled extensively to show them. He's developed a reputation for the qualities of his breeding programme and his kittens sold for good money. He also uses the name Mace, Albanian for cat. He's remained on the Albanian police radar for some years. Investigators were of the opinion he'd used the cats he travelled with as cover for the conveyance of criminal goods.'

Nash continued, 'That view was established when a wiretap on a bigger player they were watching brought Kamal and his enterprise into their investigation. Conversations about the movements of cats and cat-related goods were deciphered as code for the movement of drugs and guns. He did, or does, have an interest in the breed but his money was coming from more than first prize at a show. The crux came when detectives in Albania made the link that there were no cat shows that related to the dates and times he purported to travel for the purpose of showing or exhibiting. The conversations recorded implicated Kamal in criminality but not enough to convict him. Despite surveillance, he was never seen with anything other than a cat carrier or a winner's rosette.'

'Kamal was tipped off by a corrupt detective. Kamal left and entered the UK with his son. They were granted leave to remain despite the concerns I've highlighted. He opened and operated different businesses before he settled on the phone business he runs to this day. Vesa Ramiz is twenty-five and the son of Kamal. He's worked with his father since he was fifteen. There were no reports from Interpol in relation to Vesa but on the CRIMINT intelligence system there are protected intelligence reports.

These reports are of rumours about the shop taking in stolen phones.' Nash began to walk around the table as she considered what to divulge next.

'I don't know how this links with our murders but the association is too strong for me to ignore. This brings me to my number. I purchased the phone and SIM card from there as I always did when I needed an unregistered phone. There's something deeper going on there and we need to dive to dredge it up. I want actions initiated to establish more on the lifestyle of Kamal. I'll meet with the Homicide Task Force DI and see if his team can assist with some lifestyle surveillance. Sally, research all the Abyssinian cat breeders in the UK. See if Kamal's name crops up, or another business associated to him comes back. We need to see if his travels have continued in the UK and where Kamal's been frequenting. What breed were the cats the victims owned?' Nash asked the room, in the hope someone may have taken note.

'They were a mix of breeds. None were Abyssinian though… from the little research I conducted on cats in general,' JJ said.

'Conduct the enquiry anyway, and let's establish where and when these cats were purchased. Maybe… just maybe, Kamal has advertised having cats of any breed for sale on Gumtree or Preloved and used his business as a point of contact for people to visit him,' said Nash.

'Do you have a cat, ma'am?' Sagona spoke up from the depths of the room.

'Why do you ask, George? Don't tell me you breed the things too?' she asked.

'No, I hate them. I was confused as to how your number entered the investigation, and we seem to have skirted around this.' He sat back and placed his interlocked fingers on his mountain for a gut.

Nash imagined an empty room save for her and George, where she'd take a swing to eradicate the smart-lipped grimace he'd developed having asked the question.

She hadn't forgotten about her number. She needed to shut a few doors before she could open the one that would resolve that issue.

Nash waited for the voices that had surfaced to diminish beyond an echo.

'I'm as keen as you all are to nip that in the bud,' she said. 'Background enquiries are being conducted to ascertain how my number appeared on each of the victims' call data. I can only reiterate that I haven't had any contact with the victims. I'm determined to answer your question as much as you're determined to get an answer. Until then, we conduct all the new actions I've allocated. George will disseminate these after this meeting. They will concentrate on Kamal Ramiz. We now have three victims. Let's not come back here with a fourth.'

Nash stepped back from the table and, with a fleeting glance around the room, left for her office and the chance to call the DI to arrange the surveillance, and to give herself five minutes alone to interrogate her mind about the unhelpful thorn in her side – the link between her covert telephone number and the victims of murder.

As she entered her office she was conscious of a shadow that wasn't hers. She turned to see Clarke about to knock and she beckoned her in. Clarke sat in the comfy seat as she removed her headphones. Nash waited the customary period of time she normally did before she'd turn her attention to Clarke.

'So, how can I help you? You did a great job with the presentation and I've made a note for DS Matthews to add it to your annual appraisal,' said Nash.

Clarke stared at the floor, her cheeks flushed.

'I didn't include everything as I wanted to speak to you first. I would've spoken to DS Moretti but he said he was too busy. He always says that whenever I ask him anything, and I know he isn't as he disappears into the filing room and doesn't come out for at least thirty minutes, and never carries a file.'

She paused, then continued, 'When I was looking into the crime reports on the computer, nothing was showing up, but then I found a dispatch report that related to an abandoned call traced to Melissa's flat three months ago. I followed it up with the officer who'd attended. She explained that it was a strange call. The officer said the occupier gave her name as Melissa Phelps and said everything was all right and she'd dialled by mistake. The officer told me there was something the occupier was holding back. She tried to press her for the reason for the call, but then left as she couldn't stay any longer. It's bothered me, as Melissa appeared very much in control of all other aspects of her life from what I've found. I think a detective needs to follow it up, not with Melissa, obviously, but with her parents or work.'

As Clarke finished speaking, Nash saw Moretti drift past her door. On the way to the filing room no doubt, she thought.

'Nick,' Nash shouted.

Moretti stuck his head around the frame of the door. 'Yes, did you call my name?'

'I did. Can you contact the parents of Melissa and ask them how she was about three months ago? Had she been in contact, or talked about anything that was troubling her? I'm going to meet with the DI from the HTF, so update me as soon as you've made contact.'

Nash thanked Clarke and stood up. Clarke did the same and they both left her office and went their separate ways.

Nash found the DI for the HTF in his office. His dark beard neatly groomed to complement the slickness of his handmade suit. She coughed and he looked up.

'Pippa, a sight for tired eyes, come on in,' he said.

He stopped the work he was engaged in.

'How's tricks?' he asked, as he pointed at a freshly percolated coffee pot he'd lifted from the heated base it inhabited.

Nash nodded at the mug and he filled two. He handed her the cleanest one and she sat opposite him as she placed her mug on a small low coffee table.

'I need your team for some lifestyle work on a potential subject in my murder investigations,' Nash said. She came to the point without being blunt. She could see he was busy.

'I'd love to help, Pip, but they're all assigned on another manhunt and I can't pull them away. If I could, I would. You know that,' he said with a shrug of his broad shoulders.

Adam Sharpe was his name. Sharpe with an 'e' and his mind matched his surname. Nash was on the same DI course as him and they'd got on exceptionally well. She was glad when they'd both been posted to the Homicide Command and had hoped they'd see more of each other outside of work, but their roles were such that death didn't stop to make things easier for them.

'Why don't we do it?' Sharpe said.

Nash mused on the proposition. She wasn't an ideal candidate for surveillance as Kamal knew her by sight, but he didn't know Sharpe and right now she was running out of options. She needed Moretti at the helm while she kept the plates in the air.

'Very well. I drive and you observe. Let's see where it takes us. What time are you free?' she asked.

'Get all the written authorities in place and call me. Give me what you have on the target and we'll use one of my cars,' Sharpe said, lifting his mug in salute.

Nash got up and as she wandered back to her office, she stopped off at the filing room and entered. Moretti was sat reading a magazine. His eyes as wide as his mouth, as though he was blowing out a smoke ring.

'This all looks very comfortable, Detective Sergeant. Any pastries on offer or were you about to leave the office on the action I'd requested and bring some back once you'd made the call to the parents?' she enquired as she leaned against the steel cabinets.

'I've put the call in. It went straight to answer machine, but I left a message for them to call me back as soon as they can,' he blustered, as he searched for where to place his magazine, and settled for chucking it under his seat.

'Nice space you've got here,' Nash remarked as she surveyed Moretti's lair.

'Look, Pip – ma'am...'

'Relax. I'm not here for a fight. I don't blame you seeking solace at times. I have my own space too as it goes.'

'Oh yeah, where's that then?'

'I'm not telling you. I'd turn up to find half your shit moved in,' she said as she turned and left him to it.

Before the door closed, she looked back. 'I'm going out with DI Sharpe, so hold the fort. Call me when you hear from Melissa's parents,' she said.

Moretti jumped up and grabbed the door before it shut.

'Do I not get an invite or is it not work-related?' he asked, his mouth now downturned at the edges as though his mother had scolded him.

'It's work, and no, you don't get to come out to play. I need you here. Ensure the actions from the last scene get allocated and followed up. I'm on the phone should you need me, and stay out of that room. I need you where you can be contacted.'

With that she smiled and waved, and entered the main incident room. She found a detective on the Intelligence Desk and tasked her to write up the surveillance authority and send it back to her to get authorised. Nash would speak to her DCI in the meantime and, provided he was winning at whatever course he was on, he'd happily sign off the authorities for her and Sharpe to start their surveillance.

CHAPTER THIRTY-SEVEN

Sharpe parked away from Kamal's home address but kept them within a safe distance so they could observe the front of Kamal's property. It was a modest semi in a residential London street. Nash had called Harris who'd informed her that Kamal wasn't at the phone shop. He'd offered to put a call in to Kamal to try and establish where he was, but she'd declined the offer. Nash preferred to keep Harris out of this hunt, for now. They'd taken a gamble that Kamal would be at the address they'd established was his home. The street was serene for the time of day.

Trees lined the edge of the pavement like a parade of skeletons who sought new skin. Nash gathered her coat around her neck and pulled up a plain grey scarf over her chin. She sunk deeper into the leather passenger seat of Sharpe's fleet vehicle. An Audi estate with blacked-out rear windows.

He'd killed the engine and sat back as he comfortably glanced over at Kamal's front garden.

Research had established nothing of concern. A satellite image revealed an alleyway that ran behind the houses and the gardens at the back.

Kamal could choose to leave that way and if he did, they'd miss him. Sharpe turned to Nash who looked as though she was being devoured by the seat.

'Cold?' Sharpe enquired.

'You're not a DI for nothing, are you,' she replied, as she blew into her hands. The vapour from her breath filled the space in front of her and briefly misted the windscreen.

'How come you aren't?' she asked.

'Heated seat. Same as you, but you haven't bothered to activate it,' he said with a show of perfect teeth.

Nash shuffled to upright as she leaned forwards and ran her index finger along the base of the dashboard until she found the button for her seat. She pressed it three times and sat back and waited for the warmth to radiate through.

Sharpe chuckled to himself as he clapped his hands together and moved them as though he was starting a fire using rubbed sticks.

'Do you think he's in?' Nash asked.

'My guess is as good as yours. There's no vehicle outside and from the reports on our systems, he doesn't have access to a car. I do find that difficult to believe though,' Sharpe said.

Sharpe nodded in the direction of the front window. A curtain moved. All the windows were closed. It was a pet or a person. It could also mean Kamal had left by the backdoor and a gust of air had moved them.

As Nash and Sharpe watched the front door to Kamal's house, the sound of an engine disrupted their attention. They both turned to look to their right. The engine sounded like it needed a good tune-up, as the car rolled stealthily over the tarmac towards the junction where Nash and Sharpe were parked. Sharpe reached forwards, and his index finger hovered over the ignition button. The vehicle crawled opposite Kamal's address and stopped. Plumes of exhaust smoke continued to emit from the rear of the car.

'I hope this isn't a hit,' Sharpe mumbled into his chest.

Nash dropped the internal visor as though she was going to apply makeup and continued to observe. She looked up into the vanity mirror and hovered a used lip gloss over her lips. She rarely wore makeup and tended to carry anything of that nature for this purpose only.

They remained as unobtrusive as they could. The attention of the distant vehicle's occupants was directed towards the front door to Kamal's house. A door that was now open. Nash recognised Vesa. He looked left and right before he stepped out of the house and sauntered towards the car. The meet was swift. Nash and Sharpe recognised the hand actions indicative of an exchange masked as a greeting. Vesa was back inside in a flash, and the car drove away leaving a fog in its wake. Nash noted the index plate of the vehicle and was already on her mobile making a call to her inside team to check the index on the Police National Computer. The response was swift – no registered keeper. Nash held the screen of her phone low as she showed Sharpe the reply.

No sooner had the vehicle left than another arrived. The driver displayed the same clandestine tactics as the previous one. Vesa appeared at the door, moved his head in the same way, then, once he was satisfied his path was clear, he approached the vehicle with the same casual air as before. This time Sharpe was on his phone and leaned down as he spoke. He knew many of the borough crime squad DSs well. He spoke with an assured confidence as he conveyed exactly what he required to the person at the end of the line. Once Vesa was back inside, he sat back up.

'That was Barney Coles. He's a DS on a crime squad that covers this area. He's got a team out at the moment and they're close by. If he sees the car, they'll stop it and turn it over. Let's see if we can flush out what Vesa is so keen to offload. May as well, as my gut tells me Kamal isn't in,' Sharpe said.

There were no other cars after the last one.

Nash wasn't impressed.

'This is my operation. As much as I appreciate the help, you're my driver for this outing and I will take all the operational decisions, Adam,' Nash said.

Sharpe raised his hands from the steering wheel.

'You're right, Pip, I'm sorry. I got carried away. I'm so used to taking the lead. I can't promise it won't happen again though. If my gut reacts, I don't ignore it, but I will talk before taking action,' he replied, his face now relaxed.

Nash maintained her gaze on his.

'Good,' she said, as they returned their attention to the job in hand.

Ten minutes passed. Sharpe's phone vibrated. It was his contact, Coles.

'We've stopped the car,' Coles said.

'Go on,' replied Sharpe, keen to know the result. No matter how big or small the target of the surveillance, he loved a result. It justified the work he was deployed on, and the authorised level of collateral intrusion in the public's life that was unavoidable. 'Don't leave me in suspense, what did you find?'

Sharpe turned the phone onto speaker so Nash could hear.

Sharpe waited. He could hear Coles was still connected as a rustle of clothing could be heard, then his voice was clear.

'Sorry, I was getting back into my car before I explained more,' he offered. 'The driver had a wedge of SIM cards on him. All of them clean-looking. I would say they are cloned.'

Sharpe thanked him and looked at Nash.

'Lift him,' she said.

Coles was happy to oblige as his job had gone quiet and his team were bored.

Nash leaned away from Sharpe. He noticed her face had taken on a pallid appearance. Her once bright eyes appeared dull and she blinked as though caught in a blizzard.

'Everything all right?' Sharpe asked as he set his mobile back in the charging cradle.

'He's certain they were SIM cards?'

She'd heard Sharpe's contact as clearly as he had, but her brain buzzed and wouldn't relax until she'd had it confirmed.

'Yeah, you heard him yourself, and there's no mistaking what a SIM card looks like. Why, what's the problem? I appreciate it isn't exactly the most exciting discovery but hey, needs must,' he replied. Sharpe spoke evenly and with an air of empathy.

'Let's go,' Nash said as she drew the seatbelt across her chest and clicked it home.

Sharpe shrugged and pressed the ignition. The engine sparked to life and they moved away from their spot.

'Are you going to share with me the sudden change of heart?' Sharpe asked as he palmed the steering wheel and steadied their course. He was quite happy to call it quits.

Nash rummaged in her bag that she'd dumped in her footwell. As she placed the bag on her knees, her feet felt the benefit of the car's heater. She produced the phone she used to communicate with DS Harris.

'I can't say too much, but this outing has been very beneficial, thanks,' she said.

Sharpe remained silent.

She placed the UC phone back in her bag. DS Harris didn't need to know this aspect of her investigation, yet.

'So, where to now? Office, or do you have anywhere else I can drop you?' Sharpe said.

'The office would be great. I'll need to get my team together,' she said. 'Thanks for the help.'

'Anytime,' Sharpe replied.

They drove back in silence save for a few stilted conversations about nothing in particular, job politics and recent over-promotions. Once they were back at Hendon, Sharpe dropped Nash outside the gates and left. Nash walked across the parade square and back to her office. As she walked, she noticed the light in her own office was on.

* * *

As Nash entered her domain, Moretti looked up from her computer screen. He brushed crumbs of biscuit from her keyboard.

'I'll be out of your hair in just a minute,' he said.

Nash's glare was enough to tell him his actions weren't appreciated.

'No rush. I have something I need to run by you, so I'll get us a couple of coffees while you run the hoover over my floor,' she said.

The coffee made, they sat in her comfy chairs. The hoover hadn't been located but Nash wasn't as concerned about office hygiene as she'd made out.

'Any news from Melissa's parents?' Nash asked.

'Yes, but you go first. How was the surveillance? Any result?' Moretti replied.

Nash let the seat take the strain and brought her mug with her.

'We had a great result as it happens,' she offered.

'Wow! That's a shock. I thought it would be the usual; no show and what a waste of time that was,' Moretti said.

'A car turned up. Vesa was seen to conduct an exchange. Sharpe had the car stopped away from the area. The driver was searched. He had a collection of SIM cards on him, all appeared to be cloned.'

Nash wanted to see what Moretti made of it. She didn't need to wait long to have her suspicions confirmed.

'Well, well, well – that's answered one thing about why your number was on the victims' call logs. I also have some news that will make our case much stronger,' Moretti said. 'I had a call back from Melissa's mum. I'd probed, tactfully, as you asked. She remembered a vital piece of what we've been missing.'

Nash sat forwards.

'Go on,' she said.

Moretti reached behind him for his daybook. He opened it at the page where he'd made an entry of the conversation. He wanted to ensure he didn't forget anything.

'I asked her why she thinks Melissa may have used the phone shop rather than a regular high street phone provider. I had to allude to it otherwise I could've missed an opportunity. Her mum was apologetic, said she should've told us earlier but it had escaped her mind,' he continued.

'Melissa had phoned her up and confided that she'd been attacked while on her way home. A phone robbery by those on mopeds. Anyway, her mum suggested she get another phone and insisted she get software on it that could ensure she, her mum, knew that she was at home safely. The software was designed so that you could link trusted users, and they'd receive a safe message once the phone's owner was satisfied they were not going out again. So Melissa had the software installed. She'd send her mum a message via the app when she got home and wasn't going back out. The software also meant that if she was out, her mum could see where she was, and this brought her peace of mind. The software's used by parents to check up on their kids' location. They can have it downloaded on their phone and as long as you have the number of the other person, you can see where they are as long as the phone is on,' Moretti said.

'What was the name of the software on her phone?' Nash asked.

Moretti flicked over the page of scrawl and ran his index finger down the page until he located it.

'One minute – here it is… Got Ur Back,' he said.

Nash remembered where she'd heard of that software before. It was advertised in the window at Kamal's phone shop. Nash took out her phone and searched for the name of the software. It didn't appear anywhere on the Internet search. She tried again and included different combinations of spelling, as well as getting Moretti to use her computer to look up all similar software used to trace a person or a phone. They both came up blank. There was software that could achieve the same results, but nothing under that name.

'Why are we not finding any details about this software online?' Moretti asked. As he did, there was a tap on the door and Clarke framed the entrance.

'I'm sorry, I was on the way to the loo and couldn't help overhearing and, well, I was interested, so stayed and listened,' she said.

Nash and Moretti stared at her, then it was as though both realised who they were talking to, and they averted their gaze. As they did, Clarke continued.

'I know why you won't find it in an online search,' she said, and stopped there.

Nash knew her well enough by now to know that she wouldn't expand unless asked a direct question in response to her statement.

'Why?' Nash asked.

'Because it's unlicensed software,' she said.

As the weight of her statement sank in, both Nash and Moretti looked at each other as the pertinence of Clarke's answer hit home.

CHAPTER THIRTY-EIGHT

'Right, you lovely lot, listen up, listen up.' Nash brought her team to attention. She'd had to call them back in again and she'd reassured them that the effort was worth it. All of them responded as she'd expected them to.

'Thanks for getting back here so quickly. I know this has felt like I've had you all on a piece of elastic but, as I'm about to explain, there's a valid reason for your attendance. I couldn't have got this far without you. You've worked tirelessly under difficult circumstances. Circumstances created by Professional Standards as much as our killer.

The extraction of two key staff members in the midst of a triple murder investigation isn't easy.'

Nash moved from behind the safety of the conference table where she was sitting. She brushed her hands down her trousers and let the creases fall as she prowled the room. She was like a starving leopard. Her prey wasn't her team. Her prey lay beyond the confines of her incident room. She'd gathered her pack together concerned with one action and one action only: the takedown of Kamal's empire.

Her detectives had witnessed her passion for duty, but this time they were taken aback at the ferocity with which she conveyed it.

Nash stopped by two empty seats. She leaned on the backs of the chairs and ran her hands along the back of one as a butler would inspect for dust as she continued her address.

'I was never happy with the decision to take two valued members off my team. We're now at the stage where I need them back. We're now at the stage where the result of their work, in addition to all of yours, has culminated in the direction we need to bring the killer in. I refuse to continue without them.'

Nash was vociferous. She didn't like to rock the boat with other department heads, but the reasons why her officers weren't permitted to be with her team were petty, and amounted to a clash of egos – one which DI Richards had lost by going one rank higher to his DCI. Nash had no intention of finding hers to join the fight. She'd rather stand alone. Fall on her sword if it came to that.

There was a light knock on the briefing room door. Heads turned as DC Jones tried in vain to creep in. Behind him DS Matthews followed. The room erupted in a cheer. They stood, shocked at the welcome, and took in the adulation they'd not expected. Both their faces flushed, but then broke into wide smiles as they moved along the back wall towards Nash and their respective chairs.

As they approached her they went to shake her hand, but Nash stopped them, and in an unusual move, gave them both a brief hug before they sat down. Nash turned back to her team. This was their time. Their moment to shine, and she valued having such great people with her. When she'd looked out the window at the returning cars of detectives, prior to entering the briefing room, she'd seen heads hung low and an exhausted shuffle of feet as they'd moved from their cars to the incident room. Now they looked as though they'd been given an invite to an exclusive party.

'Thanks, ma'am. Before you begin, you should know that DS Harris was three cars back from ours at the main gate and he was remonstrating with security,' Jonesy said, as he placed a pad and pen on the table and waited for direction.

Nash smiled her thanks and cracked on.

'Right, I'll keep it succinct,' she said as she pointed the clicker at the projector screen. She clicked three times and images of each murder victim appeared. Each image showed them exiting the phone shop.

'As you can see, each of our victims had used this shop. The keen-eyed amongst you will have noticed a poster in the window. The poster is for tracking software called Got Ur Back. This is unlicensed software that we now believe is designed in-house and placed on all the smartphones they sell. It serves two purposes. I will come onto those soon. Some of you who've been engaged in follow-up calls to family and work colleagues of Melissa and Jade, will realise that they had issues of personal safety that weren't known until now. Melissa and Jade were aware they did, as they'd requested the software. Jade had a client who'd been causing her problems, and her legal firm had advised her to arrange tracking software on her phone so they could be assured she was safe and found in an emergency. They didn't stipulate where to get it from, but it's believed Jade knew of the shop from her clients, who'd said they were legitimate and offered good deals. Her management advised her to get the software elsewhere, but didn't follow up.'

'Melissa was another whose mother insisted she get it after her phone was stolen in a violent street robbery. Both victims used Kamal's shop, so they were aware of the software's existence. Our last victim, Bryony Moore, isn't as clear. According to friends and relatives, they'd no idea she had the software on her phone, which she does. Surveillance footage shows Bryony leaving the shop with a bag that contains the outline of a box that we believe contained a new mobile phone. An iPhone to be exact.' Nash paused for a beat while she looked at the screen and how it was coming together.

Her team was attentive with no desire to interrupt her flow, but the door opened again. DS Harris pointed at Nash and then behind him as he shut the door.

Nash continued.

'It's my belief that the software has been used by our killer to remotely track where each victim lived. They'd be able to choose their moment to attend and attack. They'd have access to the app that opened the door to the blocks of Jade and Melissa, and would be able to enter their flats in the same way. They'd have everything they'd need from the victim's phone. How? I'll come onto that, as well as how my covert number enters the equation. I'm now in a position to explain why I think my number appeared.' Nash paused and waited to make sure they were all up to date with note taking before she continued. This was a message she wanted them left in no doubt about. It was about her integrity as well as being part of the enquiries.

'Earlier, DI Sharpe and myself sat up outside Kamal's home address. Vesa was seen to conduct an exchange with the driver of a vehicle. The car was stopped by a local crime squad and when searched, a quantity of SIM cards was found. All of them believed to be cloned. I too have been using the same shop for my other role as a UC. It's my belief that the shop sells the original cards and deals the cloned versions. The cloned version of a SIM card I'd bought there was used by someone to make contact with each victim. That someone is our killer. That's whom we need to find, and hopefully recover the cloned SIM card at the same time, along with the phone it was in when the call was made. The phone I used with the SIM on the restricted log has a different IMEI number to the one on the billing data from the victims. In other words, it didn't come from my phone although the SIM card number showed the same.

'I said there was more than one reason as to why I'm thinking the shop is key to finding the killer. The shop is a hub for the proceeds of crime. It takes in stolen phones from many different routes, but one is robbery. Robbery of the latest models from warehouses, as well as personal robberies on the street. It's my belief that each customer is sold a phone with the software pre-installed. Kamal insists on setting up the phones for customers as part of the personal service. This enables him to remotely access each phone when it's live, and to see where the victim is. Contact is made with the robbery gang on mopeds. They are dispatched to the area where they steal the phone, bring it back to the shop for a commission, and the phone's resold to the next mug and so on. I don't know who our killer is, but I'm certain the shop is key. The way they operate means that they can easily clone a phone or remote access it once it's live. This is how they've been able to enter the victims' blocks and main flats undetected. The cloning of the phone and app for Melissa's and Jade's flats at least. Bryony's was key entry. We're going to raid the shop and Kamal's home address. First, though, I need to be certain where Kamal and Vesa are. I want them contained.' Nash finished speaking and waited for the questions.

There weren't any, and Nash was surprised as she'd taken a leap of faith with what amounted to supposition as to how the killer could access the victims and the premises. She had no proof, and she hoped the proof lay in the house or the shop. By busting the shop, she hoped one of them would confess to whom they'd been dealing with or sold the software on to, and the investigation would roll on. If they didn't then she'd ensure they'd never leave prison on anything else she uncovered in addition to DS Harris and his team. She nodded at Moretti to continue with the logistics while she left to talk with Harris.

CHAPTER THIRTY-NINE

Harris was pacing Nash's office when she entered. He stopped and faced her. She closed the door.

'So, is it true?' Harris asked.

'What?'

'That you intend to crash my party and bring unwanted guests,' Harris hissed through clenched teeth.

'Sit down before you fall down,' Nash said, as she moved behind her desk.

Harris remained in his occupied territory. Nash moved in front of her desk.

'I have three murders, Carl, and Kamal's shop is linked. I cannot and will not ignore it. Murder trumps robbery, as you alluded to, need I say more?' Nash said.

She saw no requirement to defend her actions, and if Harris took a step back from his ego, he'd realise she was right. Harris wagged his forefinger as he willed his mouth to find the appropriate words. He couldn't and had struggled to prior to his arrival.

'Look, can't we come to a compromise? How about leaving it a couple of days before you hit it? For old times' sake?' Harris said, a note to his voice Nash hadn't heard before. A child-like note that only reinforced her position.

'No. I'm hitting them today. I need to know where Kamal and Vesa are though. I'm sorry, but you've got enough to charge Kamal. A couple of days isn't going to make a huge difference either way,' Nash said.

By way of peace offering she motioned at the door with her arm. Harris wiped his hair with his sweaty palm, then ran it over his face as he let out a long breath. He turned towards the window that overlooked the parade square. He knew he didn't have a leg to stand on when it came to three murders over his robbery operation. He knew the operational team were keen to enter the arrest phase too. This meant his role was no longer necessary or proportionate, and they should go ahead and arrest and charge with what they had.

'When do you want to do this, and where?' Harris asked, calmly.

'I'd prefer both Kamal and Vesa to be at the shop,' Nash said. There was no sense of victory, just a need to get the job done.

'How about I put a call in to Kamal and arrange a meet. Kamal was asking for another one anyway, so it won't look too suspicious when it all comes on top. I'll drag you along too. That way the letch is bound to agree on the short notice and hopefully bring his sidekick of a son too. I can't guarantee that though, but it's the best I can do. You'll have to disappear before the main event though. You can't waltz in with the door crashers and hope he won't put two and two together. You're either in my way, or not at all, ma'am,' Harris said, his tongue firmly in the side of his cheek.

Nash nodded her agreement and Harris left her office closing the door behind him. She understood his logic. Her undercover role had blurred boundaries now that her murder investigations had overlapped with the covert operation. She didn't wish to show out, as was the terminology in the police, but she'd happily give evidence behind a screen, or by any other measure that protected her anonymity.

She didn't dwell on that though. She'd seek advice from counsel, and was confident a way forward could and would be found that was legal. The waters were murky enough. Only time would tell whether this was her last role as a UC, due to circumstances that were beyond her control. To bring justice for the victims was her main priority, and always would be the overriding factor in her role. Harris left her to make his calls and prepare.

* * *

She laid out the clothes for her meeting with Harris. He'd texted saying it was on. She had three hours. She'd met with Moretti and DS Matthews and briefed them as to their roles. Moretti would manage the outside team, and Matthews the inside team. She'd flicked on the radio once they'd left. Radio X back home. *How I made my Millions* by Radiohead was the song she listened to as she changed her skin as she saw it. Moretti would speak with the operational team's DS for Harris's phone job, and co-ordinate resources with them.

She took the phones, including the Nokia from Harris, from her drawer. She'd have no radio. All Moretti could do was wait to see her leave, and give it three minutes before he sent the message for the Ops team heavies to storm the building and secure the place. At the same time, another wing of the Ops team would be at Kamal's home address doing the same. Now wasn't the time for pumping beats to raise Nash's adrenaline. She noticed a dull ache in her stomach she hadn't expected.

She took her car keys from the desk along with her clutch bag and placed her phones in it. With one final sweep of the room she closed the door as the song faded into Idles' *Benzocaine*. She left the radio to play her out as she made for her car and the arranged link up with Harris.

CHAPTER FORTY

They sat in Harris's car in a side street while they watched London life flow past them. Exhaustion had crept up on Nash and as she leaned onto the doorframe, she longed for the comfort of her own living room, a takeout curry, fresh pyjamas and a decent film.

Moretti had messaged to say all was in place. Nash felt a small comfort having read that. Harris had been stoical on the journey. They'd made conversation, but he too sounded as though he needed a break from it all. A chance to kick back and be himself rather than play the criminal and live the life. He'd even spoken of retirement. A subject he rarely mentioned as it frightened him too much. He'd moan about the police, as did everyone, but he never really engaged in that type of conversation beyond the odd grunt of agreement.

'You ready?' he asked as he turned towards her.

'I'm ready,' she said, giving him a weak effort at a smile.

Harris didn't move and continued to study her face.

'Look, Pip. I'm with you on this but you appear distant. What's wrong?' Harris said as he adjusted the internal blower away from his face.

Nash didn't reply and stared out the window as she thought.

Harris continued, 'What I mean is, if we're to go down into the basement, I need to know you've got my back as much as I have yours. This is it, the final push, the team's going over the top tonight – to glory and beyond. You look as though you've been posted to traffic with no option of a return to detective duty. Cheer the fuck up will ya, and let's get this shit done. Here, have a line before we go in,' Harris said, as he reached into his pocket.

Nash's eyes snapped towards him as Harris produced a handkerchief that had seen better days and blew his nose.

'Put some decent music on and let's take five before we leave the car,' she said, opening the glovebox and riffling through various CDs that Harris stored there.

She opened a box and depressed the centre of the case. She removed the disc by the edges, displaying the fact to Harris, who nodded his approval at the handling and loaded it into the slot. She sat back as she winked at Harris and turned up the volume.

The opening guitar riff to *Highway to Hell* thundered out of the speakers and they both stared ahead. Their heads began to nod with the beat and as Harris began to play air guitar, Nash belted out the lyrics.

* * *

Moretti turned to the Ops team leader. They were sitting in a non-descript van and observed Harris's car. A car that now rocked and bounced. Moretti raised his eyebrows as did his counterpart, DS O'Dowd, from the Violent Crime Task Force, who accompanied him.

'What the fuck's going on?' O'Dowd asked, shaking his head in disbelief. 'Nash and Harris should've been in the target venue five minutes ago.'

Moretti sat back in the seat in the rear of the van.

'My guess is she's getting ready to rock 'n' roll with Harris,' he replied.

O'Dowd snorted. 'Fucking UCs,' was all he could muster by way of a reply, as they waited for them to finish and leave.

CHAPTER FORTY-ONE

Nash and Harris approached the door to the rear of the premises. An external camera dipped as the security light activated – a new addition since Harris had last visited. Harris hoped the Ops team had planned for it in their recce.

The door was opened by Vesa and they entered. Kamal was, as ever, pleased to see them and the familiar charade of a search was not insisted on. Phones were placed on the table. Nash turned off her iPhone and left the Nokia as it was.

'Why you always carry that junk Nokia?' Kamal asked her.

Nash leaned back on her chair. She placed her hands behind her neck and let out a long breath as she shook her head. The effect was instant. Kamal concentrated on her chest, which was accentuated by her stretch, and wasn't concerned by the lack of answer.

Kamal shrugged as he got up. He produced the familiar bottle of family-brewed spirit and poured three shots. Either Vesa didn't drink or wasn't invited. He'd disappeared as he always did, back to his dark room and closed the door.

Kamal clutched the glasses in a pinch. He brought the entire ensemble back to the table and set them down. They went through the formal toast and all of them knocked back the spirit.

'Now you drink?' Kamal questioned.

Harris wiped his mouth and motioned towards his glass with a nod. Kamal topped him up and showed the bottle to Nash. She pushed her glass in his direction, and he grimaced in a way that made her stomach turn.

Harris decided he'd compere the event and opened the performance.

'Thanks for seeing us at short notice,' Harris said with a raised glass.

The action was replicated by Nash and Kamal, and they settled into the meeting. The conversation was conducted with the intention of letting Kamal update them on where he was logistically, and whether this arrangement was a one-off, or if he'd set the wheels in motion for another load of phones. Nash let Harris continue as she scanned the basement in the hope of seeing anything that might assist her investigations. She felt relieved that Vesa was on the premises. She wanted the meeting over so she could depart and get some fresh air, while the joint operation swung into effect.

Harris had assured Nash he'd keep the meeting tight. Tie up any loose ends. It was also a final way of cutting Nash from the operation. Nash was moving on, and would Kamal be happy to continue working with Harris if Nash wasn't as available to meet as she had been. Kamal had no issue. He didn't question why Nash would be leaving, and Harris took this as a sign of professionalism at their working engagement. They'd all worked well together, even though Kamal's world was about to cave in with no rope to claw his way out. Nash was acting as the anchor, and prepared to let it go at a moment's notice.

It was going smoothly until Vesa reappeared. He spat out a sentence in Albanian reinforcing his words with his hands. As he continued his diatribe, he motioned with his head towards Nash and Harris. Kamal's expression had changed from one of conviviality to confusion, and then rage. Kamal reached under the table and there was the sound of duct tape tearing. The barrel of a pistol faced both Nash and Harris. Harris reacted immediately. He forced the desk into Kamal and continued to push with all his bulk; the gun now aimed high. Nash quickly assessed Harris was in control. Despite Kamal still holding the gun, he was in no position to aim it.

She lunged at Vesa, who reached above the door frame. As he did, his hand came down. A glint of steel flashed before Nash's eyes as he slashed out at her face using a butterfly knife. Nash parried and ducked, but Vesa was quick. He dodged and rolled out of Nash's way. As he did, Nash could hear Harris screaming at Kamal, asking him what the fuck was happening as they had nothing worth robbing on them. Kamal spat out the words pig, and then cop.

Harris still had Kamal pinned by the table and Kamal was no match for Harris. Nash corralled Vesa, making sure she had Harris behind her at all times. If Vesa made a move for him she would counter it.

Above them came the familiar sound of the crunch and shatter of wood and metal. Nash and Harris knew that the Ops were at the back door with specialist door opening equipment. For whatever reason, they hadn't waited for Nash to leave before starting the raid. Vesa moved his feet like a crab, while Nash remained in a loose stance, hands at her centre to protect her vital organs should he lunge at her, while she moved her feet like a boxer. Vesa kept his eyes locked on hers as he moved. All Nash could see was pure evil. A side she'd never witnessed in the brief encounters they'd had when she'd visited the shop.

Vesa rocked on his toes and feinted strikes as he did. Nash made sure her left foot was in contact with Harris's heel as she moved her right leg. If he shifted, then she knew he'd been overcome, and she'd move with him. Nash spat on the ground and this made Vesa laugh.

'Look at you! Acting all gangster. All you are is a cop, fucking whore, and now you are going to die, here, with my useless fuck of a father,' Vesa said.

He continued to move in a half circle as Nash tracked him. She wondered why he hadn't attacked sooner, and could only guess that he saw her as a worthy adversary.

'You've got it all wrong, you stupid little prick. Staying down here while it's obvious the filth are coming in is of no help to any of us. You must have another way out we can all use?' Nash said.

But Vesa seemed intent on some kind of final stand. Why he had brought his father into his venom she didn't know or care at this point, but she'd noted the reaction. There was rapid talk all in Albanian that originated from Kamal. He was still pinned by the table and had appeared to have given up, but refused to let go of the firearm. Harris remained in his position, harking back to his younger days as a number eight for the Met Police's first fifteen rugby squad. Even then, at half the size he was now, he could manage the scrum well.

His one goal was to make sure Kamal couldn't use the gun, and keep everyone on his side safe. Vesa hadn't finished and continued in English.

'I told him you were police the moment you came into this shop, with your scent of the West, all perfect hair and tits. He was like the cats he so loved, a pussy whenever you came around, and now look at him? A fool who always thought more of his beloved animals and women than his own son and business. Go ahead, kill him, do us all a favour, because I know who you are, and you won't convince me otherwise.'

As Vesa finished his speech, Nash heard Kamal yell from behind her and Harris's heel separated from hers as he pushed forwards on the table. DS Carl Harris didn't need a legion of Spartans, he just utilised his will to preserve their lives. And that was all he needed.

Kamal's yell had startled Vesa. His eyes momentarily shifted from Nash to Kamal. Nash took full advantage. She flicked her hip and as she did so, the momentum continued in a roundhouse kick that connected with Vesa's cheekbone and shattered his jaw. The knife he held interrupted her flow and she felt a sting on her shin. Above her, she heard the familiar and comforting yell of 'Police stay down, stay down,' as the operational team crashed through the basement door. Two detectives piled onto Vesa, while others did the same to Nash and Harris as well as Kamal. All of them were thrown to the floor and secured as though they were criminals. It was over. They were safe, and they had their targets secured.

Harris was the first to see the blood at the base of Nash's trousers and shoes. He'd moved his face towards Nash. His cheek hugged the floor under the sole of a detective's boot that secured his head. They were lifted up and the first to be taken upstairs. Nash was immediately taken to an ambulance, where she was placed inside with the two detectives who'd supposedly arrested her. Once the doors were closed, they whispered words of apology to her and cut the plasti-cuffs, while the ambulance staff treated her injury. A knife wound to the shin, that was deep enough to require stitches.

Nash said nothing and waited calmly, with the detectives sitting either side of her. They replaced the plasti-cuffs with a set of Quickcuffs that were loosely shut. The ambulance crew weren't to know she was a police officer.

'Where are we taking her?' a detective asked the ambulance driver.

'University College Hospital, St Thomas's is too busy,' came the reply.

Nash slowly closed her eyes, thankful for small mercies.

CHAPTER FORTY-TWO

The laceration had required fifteen stitches. Nash was sitting in her living room, her legs up on the sofa, a freshly laundered set of pyjamas on, along with the TV news. This wasn't the downtime she'd wished for. Flowers and a Get Well Soon card had been sent from the team. Moretti had been the one to deliver the arrangement, and had obviously chosen the card, as it was from the value range at Wilkinson. As were the flowers. No expense spared. She loved the gesture though, and it had made her smile. She'd been home a week.

Her eyes fell on the TV as a familiar face appeared. That of DCI Carlson. It was the first time she'd seen him since Vesa and Kamal had been charged. She dug around for the remote and found it down the side of the sofa cushion. She turned up the volume. The only way she was going to establish what had happened with her jobs was from the news. Moretti was up to his eyes as acting DI and she'd left him to concentrate on the investigation. The gift of a knife wound meant she didn't need an excuse for her absence from the rest of the enquiry.

She listened as the DCI spoke of how his team had tracked and detained a ruthless killer. A killer of three, innocent women. Women whose only crime was that they'd used the same shop to purchase phones with a home-designed, pre-installed tracing software. Software used to track and kill. The killer had targeted those who accessed their blocks and doors via an app, and they all owned a cat. Bryony Moore did not have the app installed, but she had a cat and that was enough. The DCI went on with great glee to explain how raids on both the shop and the home address of the owner revealed the software and code used to design the app, and in a bizarre twist, a trophy room of jars that contained photos and tufts of cat hair. The suspect had disrupted the CCTV system in each block by posing as a British Telecom engineer, and bluffing his way to the mains systems for each block. A set of overalls purchased on eBay, a fake ID badge, and a yellow hard hat was all that was required to provide the subterfuge necessary to delay his discovery by police. Police had been pursuing the line of enquiry, but had taken too long to make the link. When asked who'd been charged, the DCI paused while he accepted an offer of water. An act, Nash thought. He was playing up to the press.

The DCI glanced down at a sheet of paper then said the words – Vesa Ramiz. A troubled man whose rampage appeared to have been triggered by his father's lack of interest in anything he did. Vesa was a boy who'd lacked any positive reinforcement. A boy who'd craved attention, but was always going to be second in line to his father's passions – cats and women. Enquiries had now gone as far as Albania and the surrounding districts where they'd lived. Missing persons enquiries that were unresolved had now been re-opened. Nash turned off the TV. She'd seen and heard enough.

She felt tired and her leg throbbed. She reached for a bottle of paracetamol and realised it was empty. She gathered her crutches and hobbled towards the bathroom cabinet where she hoped she'd find another bottle. As she entered the hall, her own mobile phone rang. She'd turned her work ones off, and certainly the spy phone Harris had given her as she didn't trust that not to be abused. She'd been thankful of it on the day of the arrests, as Harris had instructed the Ops team leader to dial it, listen, and record all the conversation.

This had pre-empted the strike on the day of the raid. They'd seen Vesa come to the rear door and talk to a group of men. Men the Ops team leader feared were about to ambush them, so had taken the decision to strike. Vesa's early intimation of hatred towards his father had formed the basis for the interview tactics and it had paid off. Vesa was more than willing to take the attention and the credit, as well as to divulge all of his father's criminal networks and operations, in the hope of getting a reduced prison sentence. Some hope, but the interview team made no promises, and Vesa declared he would enter an early guilty plea to murder, despite his defence team's reluctance to support his decision. Vesa kept to his word and did just that on his first appearance at court. Vesa knew as well as the investigative team that they had everything they needed to link him to each victim, and more, by the coding used, and the records of which phones he'd installed the software on.

Vesa had accepted in interview that his record-keeping wasn't the most criminally minded in the world, but he wasn't thinking like a criminal. He was thinking about what he wanted, and that went beyond logic. While living abroad, he'd undertaken telecom engineer training and had used this freedom of outdoor and indoor work to stalk his victims. His activities grew from stalking to rape, and then murder. He'd practised his crimes when they'd lived in Albania and it was only the move to the UK that had suspended his desire whilst he worked with his father in the shop. A suspension that wasn't to last.

Nash found her phone and looked at the screen. It was a withheld number. She didn't usually answer these, but decided to on this occasion.

'Yes,' she said, and waited.

'Pippa, it's Adam. I'm calling on my work mobile hence the withheld number. I wondered how you were and couldn't wait for you to call me and let me know,' he said.

Nash looked in the hall mirror and the small table where she left her keys and phones below it. She moved a strand of lank hair from her forehead and tucked it behind her ear as she leaned on the crutches and tried to balance the phone.

'Hang on while I put you on speaker,' she replied, as she did so and set the phone down.

'Well? Are you surviving without the thrills of detective duty?' he asked, knowing what the truth would be, but not expecting an honest reply.

'I feel like shit, if you must know. That arsehole of a DCI is on every TV and radio channel taking all the credit for my team's work, while I'm here with Lorraine fucking Kelly and *Bargain Hunt*. How about you?' she asked.

She adjusted her hair again and contemplated a shower as it shouldn't affect the stitches. She sat down on a small stool as her leg began to throb.

'I'm good, thanks. I've decided to take a week off… I wondered if you fancied a break too… separate rooms, or not… but you know, I'll look after you: food, wine, films and my enigmatic charm,' Adam Sharpe said.

He waited for what he felt was an eternity as he listened to static.

'Where are you now?' she asked.

'I'm sat in the car outside your place with both heated seats on,' he said.

Nash's eyes opened wide as she bit her top lip. She paused for a beat and scanned her flat. She'd seen cleaner squats.

'Where are you going?' she asked.

'Wherever you like. Schools aren't out so there are plenty of cottages available at short notice,' he said.

'I like Scotland. Somewhere remote where we won't be disturbed by the TV, the radio or a phone… I'll hobble down in thirty minutes. I'll be travelling light,' she said.

'I'll make some calls then; and, Pip…'

'Yes,' she said.

'I'm looking forward to being with you,' Sharpe said.

'I should hope so,' she replied, a lightness to her voice as she killed the line and turned off her phone.

Nash packed light and managed the holdall without help. She got into Sharpe's Porsche Cayenne and placed the bag on the rear seat. Once in the car, she drew the belt across her and breathed in deeply. She angled her head towards him. He raised his eyebrows and returned the smile. He activated the satnav with his voice and the screen declared their final destination: a remote getaway in Dumfries and Galloway. No Internet, phone signal or 4G. It had a landline but it was only for incoming calls and emergencies. If they needed anything the nearest shop was a three-mile drive away. Sharpe had taken a gamble and shopped for two before he'd called her. He was taking a break anyway, but whether it was with her or alone he hadn't known.

'Ready?' he asked.

'Yes; thank you. It's the best call I've taken in a long time,' she said.

Sharpe smiled back at her and with a light squeeze of her hand, they set off. Nash was happy to see the back of London. No phones, detectives or death. Only the mountains and sea air of Scotland.

If you enjoyed this book, please let others know by leaving a quick review on Amazon. Also, if you spot anything untoward in the paperback, get in touch. We strive for the best quality and appreciate reader feedback.

editor@thebookfolks.com

ALSO IN THIS SERIES

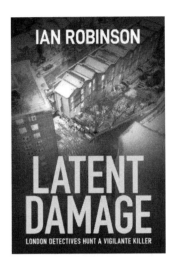

When a respected member of the community is murdered, it is not the kind of knife crime London detectives DI Nash and DS Moretti are used to dealing with. Someone has an agenda and it is rotten to the core. But catching this killer will take all of their police skills and more.

OTHER TITLES OF INTEREST

NO AGE TO DIE by John Dean

When a dangerous convicted felon is released from prison, DCI Blizzard makes it clear he is unwelcome on his patch. But when a local church takes the man in, Blizzard has to deal with the community uproar. When a local youth is killed it will take all of the detective's skills to right a wrong.

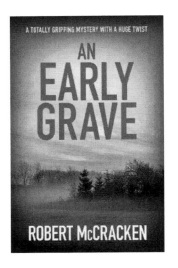

AN EARLY GRAVE by Robert McCracken

A tough young Detective Inspector encounters a reclusive man who claims he holds the secret to a murder case. But he also has a dangerous agenda. Will DI Tara Grogan take the bait?

Printed in Great Britain
by Amazon